BLACK BEACH

STEWART CLYDE

HUNT PRESS

Published by Hunt Press in 2020.

First published in 2020 by Hunt Press.

First published in Great Britain.

For Ema

"Igitur qui desiderat pacem, praeparet bellum."
If you want peace, prepare for war.

– Publius Flavius Vegetius Renatus

CHAPTER ONE

REPUBLIC OF EQUATORIAL VARRISSA, WEST AFRICA

He felt uneasy about the whole thing. He'd felt uneasy before they boarded the flight and he felt uneasy now.

He stared unblinking at the flashing wing light of the private jet. The flashes of white light lit the tops of heavy storm clouds as they cruised south over Africa. He took short, shallow breaths through his mouth and his thoughts scrambled, like static on a radio. His knee bounced and he chewed the inside of his cheek. Too many people knew the plan and there were too many things that could go wrong.

"Lord Langdon?"

The private secretary touched his knee under the table and Langdon twitched at the interruption.

"I am sorry, sir, but the President would like to discuss his arrival once more."

"He isn't the President, yet," Langdon blurted and his mind snapped back and he caught himself.

1

"Yes, sir. I understand. Excuse my presumptiveness."

Langdon looked into the round, humble, shiny black face that smiled back at him.

As docile as a Hindu cow, Langdon thought. The African adjusted his spectacles and smiled again. His toothbrush moustache, only as wide as the indentation on his top lip, twitched as he did and made him look like a black leader of the Third Reich.

"Never mind, Simeone. Excuse me. I was rash," Langdon said.

It was out of character for Lord Langdon to be anything other than charming and cool. Many years of boarding school, a military grounding at the Royal Military Academy Sandhurst, and now, accustomed to the connections and profile of those in positions of power, he seemed to glide through life, just like the private jet he sat on, as it cruised above the storm clouds.

He felt untouchable.

"A quick meeting with the boss," Langdon said to Digger Gibson. Digger was part of Langdon's security detail and had become his friend over many years working together. Digger looked across the aisle from behind his newspaper. Lord Langdon rolled his eyes and Digger gave him an apologetic look. Langdon eased himself out of the puffy white leather seats and swayed with the turbulence as he made his way towards the cockpit.

As he neared the front, the private secretary pushed past him and straightened up and tapped on the door. The secretary twisted the handle and ushered Lord Langdon into the brightly lit cabin. Langdon pulled on the lapels of his cream linen suit and smoothed the creases on the jacket. He twisted the signet ring on his pinky finger and ran a hand through his hair.

It was long and curled at the ends, more playboy than politician.

"Mister President, may I present, the Lord Langdon," the secretary announced.

"Ah, yes! My esteemed advisor, please come in," the deep rumble of a voice said.

The man who spoke the words was supposed to be the future President of the Republic of Equatorial Varrissa. An ink blot of a country in west Africa, rich in oil, and whoever ruled it, would soon be rich in mineral wealth from its mines too.

Lord Langdon bowed his head and stepped in. Apollo Koboko grinned up at him. He was spread out on a double bed, and wore the bright coloured traditional African dress of his country. He was a wheezing, obese man, and had two of his harem on the bed with him. They stroked him playfully and giggled. One pushed an oversized red grape into her mouth and chewed it with her mouth open. The room smelled of sour milk and Langdon held his breath.

"Come in Lord Langdon," Koboko said and swung an arm out in a slow arc, as if he was presenting his kingdom.

Langdon propped himself on a stool, behind a coffee table beside the bed. His knees were near his ears and his suit trousers pulled tight and up high around his ankles. There was a map of Equatorial Varrissa and piles of scattered documents and papers spread out over the coffee table.

"How may I be of assistance your Excellency?" Langdon asked and subjugated himself. Koboko was visibly pleased at the white man's prostration.

"Tell me about my arrival, will there be a military band, an escort?"

"No, your Excellency," Langdon said bluntly.

The concubines looked shocked and recoiled, and then vigorously stroked Koboko's gown with furrowed brows and looked at Langdon expectantly.

"What do you mean?" Koboko asked with a subdued fury,

"Am I not the triumphant ruler returning to my people? A Caesar back from his campaigns in the east?"

"You are, of course," Langdon said. He felt exasperated. He took a breath and calmed himself, "As I have tried to explain, Excellency, this is a delicate operation, with many moving parts. We are arriving before dawn. The private security soldiers will ensure a Palace coup. We will arrive at the Presidential Palace, *after* it is captured. This is the moment. No sooner. Everything hinges on Mabosongo signing over power, *peacefully*."

"A peaceful transition of power," Koboko mused and ran his fingers behind one of the concubine's ears. She looked away sheepishly.

"And then, I can have my parade?"

"Yes, sir, absolutely," Langdon said and the relief washed over him. "The PR agencies in London are ready and waiting to announce your triumphant return to the world. It will be a great statement, for a great statesman. You are the returning hero. The rightful ruler."

"The rightful ruler. Yes. Yes," Koboko said and grinned. His brick coloured gums showed. "Tell me more," he said and put the girl's hand on his crotch.

Lord Langdon swallowed and looked down and rubbed his eyebrow to block the view.

"Well, sir, we have many things to discuss. Your first act as President will be to assign the drilling and mining rights, as we have agreed. And then, the whole world will be your oyster. Davos, a speech at the United Nations, a Chinese delegation will visit in the coming months, and then, a world tour, military parades, women, you name it, Excellency."

"I don't like oysters Lord Langdon," Koboko said and looked at the girl as she massaged his manhood.

"Caviar then," Langdon said bluntly.

Just then, the captain's voice came over the intercom

announcing their descent into an airstrip in the remote interior of the country.

"Oh, thank Christ," Langdon said under his breath.

Koboko pushed the girl off and rolled himself over to get up.

"I must get ready," he said.

Langdon pulled the cabin door open and pushed past the private secretary and marched back to his seat.

"Bloody hell," he said loudly enough for Digger to hear and gave a sniff. "Let's just hope we can control that buffoon once he is in power."

Digger folded the paper and placed it on the table in front of him. He was relaxed. He'd seen it before and knew his role.

"Aye, boss. Let's just make sure we get him into power first, eh?"

Lord Langdon stared out the window again and calmed himself. He watched as they descended through the clouds and emerged into the early dawn sky of west Africa.

———

THE JET TOUCHED down and taxied smoothly down the runway. The seatbelt light chimed off and the air hostesses got up and moved to the exit door. Digger nodded to Lord Langdon and climbed out of his seat. He made his way to the front. The air hostesses looked him and up and down and smiled. He pulled his pistol out of his shoulder holster and checked it again, just to be sure.

They were only a small group onboard. It consisted of Lord Langdon, several of Apollo Koboko's hangers-on and entourage, and himself. Digger had seen it all in the years since he left the Special Forces and become a gun for hire. He'd served under Langdon in Libya, that was before he became 'Lord Langdon'.

It was a natural fit. He was well paid, he kept on top of the security and made sure no-one interrupted the pipeline of opportunities that made Lord Langdon and his offshore 'strategic risk consultancy' business rich.

The jet came to a halt and Digger cocked his weapon. The air hostess smiled nervously and looked at him. He nodded and she lifted the handle and the door opened. The stairs unfolded and Digger felt the chill of fresh African air. The air hostess tottered away in her heels. Digger raised his handgun and leaned around the edge of the doorway and cleared the open space. Digger looked down, and stood there, with hands-on-hips was Rex Maelstrom. A row of black Range Rovers parked behind him.

"Alright old-timer?" Rex threw a bright white smile at Digger.

"Aye, I'm alright you snotty nose bastard," Digger said and leaned around the open door to get an idea of where they were, "Any problems you amateur piece of shit?"

Rex shook his head and stepped forward.

"No, no problems, until I saw your fugly mug," he said and flashed a grin.

"Close your mouth before you give our position away with those things," Digger said and dipped his head back into the aircraft to give the all clear. And then he heard the *snap* of a bullet. He ducked instinctively and looked back at Rex. *Negligent discharge*, was his first thought - someone had fired accidentally.

"Did one of your blokes N.D.?" Digger yelled, but Rex was in a crouch looking for the source. And then there was the rolling sound of shouts and ululations and engines revving.

"We're under attack!" Digger yelled at Rex, "Get your blokes firing!"

The stewardesses screamed and Digger took a knee in the

doorway and fired at the shapes that moved in the dull light. Bullets hissed over the aircraft and thumped into the sides of the convoy vehicles.

"Digger, what the hell is going on?" Langdon shouted.

Digger heard him, but he continued to fire at the swarm of camouflage clad African rebels headed towards them.

Then he heard the unmistakable *whoosh* of a rocket fire.

"RPG!" he screamed.

Rex dived to his right and his men scattered for cover. The rocket propelled grenade's trailing smoke swirled. It hit the black sedan in the middle of the convoy. The grenade detonated in a flash of orange fireball and the force threw Digger back into the jet. The air hostesses and concubines screamed again and Simeone's mouth gaped like a fish and he whined as he lifted Digger up by the collar. The others were on the floor, in between the seats and covered their heads with their hands.

Digger scrambled backwards and Simeone screamed. The sound of automatic gunfire clattered and reverberated around them. Digger smelled cordite and heard the shouts and screams of men under fire. His instincts told him to crawl into a ball and wait for it to be over. That feeling never left. No matter how many times he was shot at. It was something to be overcome. To get up and fight back, no matter the fear. He got on one knee and leaned out again, and brought his weapon up. Shapes moved in the darkness. Fire burned on the convoy of vehicles. Men shouted and engines revved.

Someone shouted, "Grenade!"

Digger dived back inside. "Get down!" he yelled. "Grenade!"

It was a sickening sound. The heavy, dull thud of the explosion. The shockwave ran through his body and made him feel ill. He heard the fizzing sound of phosphorus burning and the high pitched screech of a man's skin on fire.

7

He wretched. Then a dark shape burst through the open door and into the fuselage. The big African stuck the barrel of an AK-47 into Digger's face and pushed him with force back to the deck. Digger saw a disorderly group of rebels pile through the door and into the aircraft. They swarmed and scattered like a disturbed nest of army ants. They pointed weapons and screamed at the passengers and dragged them into the aisle.

"Your men are dead! You must surrender!" one shouted.

Weapons stopped firing and the shouts quietened. A hush came over the cabin. An African man, slim and short in stature, wearing a black beret and olive bush shirt stepped aboard.

"Squad, shun!" one of the rebel hijackers commanded, and the soldiers slammed their heels into the deck and stood straight and upright and to attention. The man took his black beret off his afro hair and rolled it up like a newspaper he was going to use to smack a puppy.

He sank to his haunches in front of Digger and leaned in.

"Are you Lord Langdon?" he asked.

Digger shook his head, "No."

"Well, where is he, please?"

He seemed polite, but also like he was holding it together. Digger twitched his head to where Lord Langdon lay in the gangway. The man stood and grinned. He opened his arms in welcome.

"My dear Lord Langdon, welcome to the Republic of Equatorial Varrissa! This is your captain speaking, eh?" he looked around at the soldiers standing to attention, and they chuckled in a show of amusement, and then went back to their steely glares.

"I am McArthur Gentry, you might have heard of me? I am the right and true leader of this beautiful country, our home, God's home, Equatorial Varrissa!"

He looked around again and one of the soldiers started a chant, and others joined in, "Gentry, Gentry, Gentry!"

Gentry patted the air to quieten them. "Stand up please," he said and lifted an arm to one of his soldiers in the aisle. The soldier bent down and lifted Lord Langdon by the collar of his jacket. The lanky Langdon stood, head bowed and still touched the cabin ceiling. He dusted himself off.

Even hunched, Langdon looked down at Gentry.

"Well, what's all this about, Gentry?" Langdon said.

Gentry ignored him and turned back to Digger.

"And, my helpful friend, where is the fat man?" Gentry said.

Digger jerked his head the other way and Gentry smiled. Gentry took out a white handkerchief and dabbed his brow and moved to where Koboko was. He disappeared into the cabin.

Digger heard a shriek from the prostitutes and Gentry slammed the door behind him. Everyone in the plane was silent and held their breath. The soldiers looked at one another. And Digger watched Langdon. Langdon twisted his pinky ring like he was trying to polish it. He looked nervous. Digger knew that Langdon hadn't been confident about this mission. And Digger was worried about Rex and the private security outside. They were too quiet.

The only noise came from behind the closed door. Muffled tones at first, which grew. There was a thud and another scream and Gentry came back pedalling out of the cabin. Koboko came out next and charged at him like a rhino.

Gentry laughed as he back-pedalled.

Koboko heaved and pushed him with his head and chest. The soldiers moved out of the way and then grabbed onto Koboko. They couldn't stop his charge.

And Gentry just laughed. The soldiers held onto Koboko's shoulders and another went up behind him and got him in a choke hold. Koboko slowed and his breathing was heavy and rasped.

"You're going to have a heart attack, you fat bastard!"

9

Gentry goaded and Koboko shrieked and tried to move forward, but he was weighed down.

"Sergeant Bunting?" Gentry yelled.

"Yes, sir," came the call from outside the aircraft.

"Get these prisoners out of here, and get ready to move."

"Yes, sir."

"And bring me the gun of Dirty Harry."

Digger saw another man appear in the doorway, Sergeant Bunting was a tall, wry African with a sharp, long face and smooth coffee coloured skin.

If he wasn't an African guerrilla, he'd be on a runway in Paris or Berlin, Digger thought.

Sergeant Bunting's voice was as smooth as his skin and he calmly ordered the soldiers to take the prisoners outside. Gentry walked up to Bunting. He was much shorter and looked him in the eye. Gentry took the chrome Smith & Wesson handgun from Sergeant Bunting and walked past him and down the stairs.

Koboko was hauled off the plane. He fought against the weight of the skinny soldiers. They held him and swayed back and forth as he resisted and managed to walk him out the cabin and down the stairs.

Digger got himself up onto his elbow and was lifted from under the armpit by a rebel soldier. Digger waited for Langdon to come down the gangway and when he was nearby moved to walk next to him.

"What the hell is going on, boss?" he asked.

"I have no idea, Digger, no idea. But it isn't good," Langdon said and was poked with a barrel in the chest. He raised his hands in submission, "Okay, okay."

As they walked down the airplane stairs in single file, they saw the Range Rovers. They were contorted shapes of black metal and the wreckages smoked. Rex's body was lying on its side behind the lead vehicle with a halo of blood around it. The blood shone and glimmered in the light.

A fleet of old Land Rover Defenders waited for Gentry's soldiers.

Digger heard someone wailing. He looked over. He saw Koboko on the tarmac. He was on his knees with his hands strapped behind his back. Koboko sobbed and cried loudly. Gentry stood behind him. He held the Magnum to the back of Koboko's head. He spoke to him, but Digger couldn't make out what he was saying. Koboko saw Langdon making his way down the stairs and yelled out.

"Help me! My advisor, Lord Langdon, help me, please. I need you!" he pleaded and sobbed.

"Let us pray!" Gentry said loudly.

The soldiers stopped where they were. Some made the sign of the cross, they touched their foreheads and their shoulders. Everyone stopped, some closed their eyes and bowed their heads. Digger and Langdon watched with open mouths. Gentry pulled the hammer back and it clicked.

"Let his children be fatherless, and his wife a widow. Let his children wander about and beg; and let them seek sustenance far from their ruined homes. May they be blotted out of the book of life, and may they not be recorded with the righteous. O that Thou wouldst slay the wicked, O God; depart from me, therefore, men of bloodshed. For they speak against Thee wickedly, and Thine enemies take Thy name in vain. Do I not hate those who hate Thee, O Lord? And do I not loathe those who rise up against Thee? I hate them with the utmost hatred; they have become my enemies."

Koboko cried and begged.

"Amen," Gentry said.

"No, no, no!" Koboko cried out.

Gentry yanked on the trigger and the heavy revolver crashed like a thunderclap. Digger and Langdon flinched. The side of Koboko's head exploded like a watermelon. The force pushed his head forward and his heft and his body rolled forward to the tarmac. The gunshot reverberated around the vehicles and echoed into the trees.

"Amen!" The soldiers around them echoed and immediately carried on with their duties and moved the prisoners towards the waiting vehicles.

CHAPTER TWO

THE CLUBHOUSE, LONDON

Gerry Soames stuck his index finger under his collar and twisted his head for some relief from the heat. The Director of Intelligence's private secretary looked at him sympathetically as she cut open an envelope. He gave her a polite smile. His cheeks were flushed crimson and he dabbed a white handkerchief on his brow. It was an usually hot summer. The air was stagnant in London. The Clubhouse was in an old building near the river. In some rooms the exposed pipe heaters were still on.

The intercom buzzed on the secretary's desk and she daintily pressed a well manicured fingernail to turn it off. She stood up and smoothed her yellow skirt and indicated the double door that led to Sir William Alexander-Young's office, like an air hostess pointing out the exits.

Soames stood with a huff and stuffed his hanky back inside his suit jacket. His bottom jaw jutted forward and he gave her another bulldog-like smile and moved toward the doors.

"Any idea what this is about?" he grunted and she shook her head.

She tapped a knuckle on the door and pushed it open. She stood aside and held it open for Soames who walked in. He nodded his thanks as he passed.

Sir William sat behind his desk. The blinds were mostly drawn on the floor-to-ceiling glass windows that overlooked the river and London Bridge. There were two other men in the Intelligence Director's office. One was Soames' height and weight. He stood to the side of Sir William's desk. He was balding and wore a double-breasted suit, like Soames, and Soames recognised him. The other was much younger, with round-rimmed spectacles and a thick head of combed over brown hair. He was fiddling with a large rectangular screen in front of the desk. Soames had never seen him before.

Sir William was talking to the older man, Soames couldn't hear what he was saying, he only made out the word 'dispensable' as he entered.

Sir William turned his high-backed leather chair and faced Soames.

"Gerry, come in! Here, let me introduce you," Sir William said.

"Just talking about me?" Soames asked with a grin.

"Sorry?" Sir William said and raised his chin. Soames shook his head and dropped the corners of his mouth to indicate it was 'nothing'.

Sir William indicated the man to his left, "This is Mark Barkin, Chief Financial Officer for Vail Corp."

Barkin nodded and Soames said, "How do you do."

The young man at the screen turned and smiled and Sir William said, "And this is the Director of Exploration at Earth-eye, Nigel Dodder."

"Pleased to meet you," Dodder said.

"Right, let's get right to it, shall we?" Sir William said.

Soames stood in front of the desk and breathed through his mouth and his bottom jaw stuck out. He dabbed his forehead. It seemed like Sir William was dispensing with the customary five minutes of chit-chat; and to Soames' annoyance no-one was even going to mention the heat or the weather.

"The reason we are here, Gerry, is that there has been a bit of an incident in the Republic of Equatorial Varrissa," Sir William said and glanced at Barkin.

It sounded like the kind of place you learn about in school and then forget ever existed until one day it suffers an earthquake and celebrities go on television to fundraise for a relief effort.

Soames nodded. *If you're going to dispense with the small talk, just get on with it you toff*, he thought.

Sir William Alexander-Young was the type of smart social climber whose family knew all of the right kind of families and spent their winter seasons at exclusive Swiss resorts making business deals over two-thousand dollar bottles of Champagne. Sir William was in the position he was because of who he went to school with at Eton, but he was still bitter about not being the Chief of Intelligence at the Secret Intelligence Service. Merely a Director at the specialist operations division they called 'the Clubhouse'.

Soames didn't ski.

"What kind of incident?" he asked.

Sir William looked at the other two men in turn and chose his words. As he started speaking again, Barkin and Dodder both looked at Soames.

"This has to be handled with kid gloves, Gerry. This goes no further than these four walls," Sir William inhaled, held it for a second and blurted, "the Prime Minister's son, Lord Langdon, has been kidnapped in Equatorial Varrissa."

Sir William paused and his mouth opened and his

15

eyebrows raised with expectation as he watched for Soames's reaction. Soames furrowed his eyebrows and lifted the handkerchief in his clenched first to his mouth. The questions poured in like a jug under a water tap.

Who else knows? What was he doing there? What are they asking for? When did this happen? What the hell are we doing about it?

"Does the Prime Minister know?" Soames asked and scratched his forehead.

Barkin and Dodder shook their heads and Sir William said, "No, she doesn't. And we want to keep it that way. For now at least."

Soames opened his mouth to speak, but no words came. He wanted to immediately express his confused outrage, but the words stuck at the top of his throat and wouldn't come out.

"Bloody hell," Soames finally managed and felt his cheeks flush, and not from the heat.

Sir William looked up at Barkin and their eyes locked. Soames was still shaking his head when Sir William said, "Look, Gerry, we have a plan. There is a way around this."

"You've decided not to go through or over?"

Silence.

"Who kidnapped him?" Soames asked forcefully.

"McArthur Gentry," Sir William said.

"You mean McArthur 'I'm-a-cannibal' Gentry?"

Sir William nodded.

"Bloody hell."

Soames started to pace. Sir William wanted to laugh, but he leaned forward with open palms and said, "We need your operative, Gerry, what's-his-name from the Kabazanov executive action ... the Boatman."

Soames stopped pacing and looked at Sir William, he took his closed hand away from his mouth.

"Hunt," he said.

"Yes, we have a plan for a rescue mission slash covert operation to get Scratcher back."

"A rescue mission?"

Sir William nodded.

"In west African jungle?"

"Yes."

"It's a bloody war zone! What are Gentry's demands?"

"He wants us to overthrow the long serving dictator, and our current ally, and install him as President for life," Sir William said.

"And if we —"

"He is threatening to decapitate the PM's only son on video and sell the images to the highest bidder from the world's media," Sir William said, answering the question before it was asked.

"And I am guessing Mister Barkin and Mister Dodder are part of the plan for the rescue operation?" Soames asked and waved a finger between the two suits.

Sir William nodded.

"President Debby Mabosongo has put a mining conces-sion out to tender. The Russians, Chinese, Germans and others have, or are, sending teams out for geological survey. The first team to find evidence of mineral wealth wins the concession and the drilling rights. We will send your opera-tive in, undercover, as part of the security detail with the survey team, and he'll be the only one who knows the true purpose of the mission. Once in country they track down Gentry's base and rescue the hostages, and eliminate the hostage taker in the process."

"So ..." Soames thought, "Vail Corp is the money, they fund the operation, and get the drilling rights when they win, with our help?"

"That's what I like about you guys," Barkin said in a drawl, "you intelligence guys are just as smart as a tack."

Soames nodded. Barkin was American and it was starting to make sense to him. Although he still had questions.

"But, who are you?" he asked and indicated Dodder.

"Ah, I am from Earth-eye, we're a Geo-spatial Information provider that fuses multi-resolution earth observation data with advanced analytics and geo-spatial expertise to provide near-real time actionable insights."

Soames slowly nodded and smiled for the first time.

"They've got the satellites, Gerry. Earth-eye can give us dedicated satellite imagery of the whole country, and help us search for Gentry's lair."

"And I am guessing that Vail owns Earth-eye," Soames said.

Dodder looked down and stepped from foot to foot as Barkin narrowed his eyes and said, "Vail are minority shareholders in a very exciting young satellite imaging company and we've offered our services to you and Her Majesty's Government in a mutually beneficial manner."

"They're the cover, Gerry," Sir William said with a little too much emotion and protest in his voice, "they're the survey and expedition specialists. We need them to get Hunt in country and, ah, *deal* with the threat."

"Here, let me show you," Dodder said in an attempt to cut the tension and he indicated the screen with his hand. He flicked it on and showed a satellite image. Soames studied it for some time.

"It's remarkably clear," Soames said.

"Yes, this," Dodder said with pride, "is the very latest in satellite imaging technology."

"It's the future, Gerald, here and now," Sir William said, "get used to it. Space-based intelligence gathering."

"Yes," Dodder said, "As well as, of course, numerous civilian uses, like coastal sea monitoring for erosion, traffic monitoring and management, ah, port activity."

"You mean spying on other countries from space, don't

you?" Soames asked rhetorically, "in high definition technicolour."

"A much higher resolution than that," Sir William said matter-of-factly.

Dodder looked embarrassed.

"Show him the video," Sir William said to Dodder.

It was night and a bird's eye view from the satellite. On the screen a stilted video played and showed a passenger jet with some other vehicles parked parallel and nearby. Then a flash and a fireball. Other vehicles arrived in shot and after some time they drove off. The satellite zoomed out, and the picture froze.

"They were attacked? What was Lord Langdon doing there, Bill?" Soames asked.

Sir Williams' face hardened and he sat back in his chair ever so slightly. Soames knew he hated that nickname. He called him it anyway.

"That's confidential, 'need to know'," the Director of Intelligence said, "and you don't need to know."

The silence was uncomfortable and Dodder lifted his finger to say something. Soames and Sir William stared at one another and their faces hardened further.

"How is it that you had a private company's surveillance satellite overflying the exact area where the kidnapping took place?" Soames asked.

"You don't need to know," Sir William said again and cocked his head to the side, challenging him to keep going.

"Just get your blunt instrument, get the operative briefed, and get him over to Earth-eye headquarters to start the planning. I want them in country in ninety-six hours," Sir William said and his hand hit the desk like a gavel.

"Gotta find him first," Soames said.

"Well then, find him," Sir William said, "he is still government property. That'll be all. See yourself out."

CHAPTER THREE

Hunt looked down at the faded black-and-white photograph of his mother. She was young and beautiful and stood next to his equally young and handsome looking father. He guessed that it was taken soon after they'd first met. She wore a white skin-tight leotard and tutu and smiled widely. She looked happy. His father looked a bit stunned, like he'd just hit his number at the roulette table.

Hunt knew she'd been a famous ballerina in the Soviet State. Rare for someone from the Baltic Sea. She was Estonian, and the expanding borders of the Russian Federation had swallowed her nation up like fog rolled in off the sea. As a dancer and a prodigy, she'd been sucked into the vacuum of the state apparatus that used ballet as politics during the Cold War.

Hunt held the photograph up and compared it with the building across the street. He counted the ornately carved columns and the row of white statues stood on the balcony that ran around the front of the facade. Even though it was blurred and obscured in the photograph, he was sure this was where the photograph was taken.

He was sitting at a cafe across the street from the Hungarian State Opera House in Budapest. He didn't know what he hoped to find. He only knew he needed to know the truth about what happened to her. He knew she'd been taken away from her parents and moved to Moscow where she danced with the Bolshoi Ballet company. He knew that she'd met his father while they were in Hungary, and she'd defected a year later in London.

Hunt put some money on the table next to his stained espresso cup and shifted the metal chair backwards to leave. The metal legs grated against the smooth marble under an arched alleyway and the rasp echoed off the cold stone walls.

As he moved to stand he felt a heavy hand on his shoulder. The first thing he felt was the twinge of raw pain under his shoulder blade against the weight of the hand. A reminder from the man who'd stabbed him in the back. The same man who'd killed his father. And whom Hunt had left dying on the deck of a yacht in the Mediterranean.

Hunt cocked his head over his shoulder and went to grab and twist the hand on his shoulder. He saw the faded gold signet ring and turned to look.

"Sit back down old boy, they're watching us," Soames said.

"Hell, Gerry, what are you doing here?"

Soames stood up and moved around and sat at Hunt's table with his back to the Opera House.

"Well, a lovely surprise to see you too," Soames said with a wink.

Hunt suppressed a grin. Soames removed his wide-brimmed fedora and dropped it on the steel table.

"Happy to see me?" Soames asked. "Bit nippy in here isn't it?"

"How did you find me?"

"Well, aren't you even going to say hello?"

"What are you doing here, Gerry? How did you find me? Who's watching us?" Hunt asked.

Soames sat in silence for a moment. The waiter came over and asked if they wanted anything to drink. Soames ordered a bottle of sparkling water. Hunt waved his hand to indicate he didn't want anything. The waiter left and Hunt sat forward and leaned on his elbows.

"We intercepted a communication from Hungarian Special Intelligence to their brothers in the Russian Foreign Intelligence Service, about a potential British spy snooping around Hungary. They're onto you, Stirling," Soames said and glanced past Hunt's shoulder.

Stirling twirled his empty coffee cup on the table between his hands.

"And," Soames continued, "the Russians informed the Chechens that someone they might be interested in talking to was on a sightseeing tour of cultural sites in Budapest."

Stirling raised his eyebrows and exhaled and grinned.

"Well, thanks for coming, it's good to see you, Gerry."

Soames sat back and settled into his chair.

"So, where have you been Stirling?" Soames asked. "We've missed you at the Clubhouse."

"I could ask you the same thing."

"You left us, didn't you?"

"You didn't exactly give me much of a choice," Stirling said.

"Well, I am here now. You called and I came," Soames said, serious now. "What were you doing snooping around here, anyway?"

"Just looking for something."

Hunt watched Soames face. Did he really not know? He still wasn't sure if he could be trusted.

"Kabazanov told me something before he died," Stirling

said, and watched Soames face for a reaction. Soames eyes narrowed and he plucked at his roll of double chin. He checked his watch and looked over his shoulder.

"Expecting someone?" Hunt asked, but Soames didn't answer. Rather, he watched the waiter intently. The waiter had a concerned look on his face. He stood motionless and watched the dark, far end of the railway tunnel that Hunt and Soames were sitting in. Hunt glanced over his shoulder and saw the waiter, and then turned. He saw two men, heavyset in brown leather jackets, ambling towards them. But they seemed too casual and tried too hard to not look in Stirling's direction. Just then a black sedan screeched to halt on the road outside the archway.

"That's us Stirling, time to go," Soames said and grabbed his hat.

The two men froze when they saw the car and looked directly at Stirling. One of the men closest to them shouted something in Hungarian and another man appeared in the archway entrance, between Soames and the car.

"Come on," Hunt said and grabbed Soames and pulled him up by the fabric on his sleeve. They stood and made their way for the open air of the entrance. The other man rushed up to block their path. Hunt got in front of Soames and grabbed the blocker. Hunt twisted him around and held him fast by the collar. The man fought, smashing Hunt's arms to get himself free, but Hunt had him in an iron-rod grip and pulled him along behind them towards the waiting vehicle.

The two men behind him drew their weapons and yelled at him to stop and get on the ground. They fired a round over Hunt and Soames' heads. The shot clanged and echoed around the railway arches. Soames hurried ahead and pulled the rear door open and climbed in. Hunt stopped just before the car and stood square and faced the man in his grip. Hunt rocked his head back and smashed his forehead onto the bridge on his nose. The brown haired Hungarian dropped at his feet. Hunt pulled the car door shut and the they sped off and swerved into the traffic. Hunt breathed hard and turned back to see the two men from the tunnel help the other off the ground.

Hunt looked at Soames next to him in the back seat and laughed.

"You know you always have such a mischievous look on your face Captain Hunt. You always look like you have a secret, whenever I see you, you always look like you're up to something," Soames said with a smile, his face flushed red.

"That can't be good for a spy," Hunt said. "The only reason you think that is because *you're* always up to something, Soames, like a Cheshire Cat toying with a mouse."

Soames patted Hunt on the knee and checked his watch again.

"Anyway, like I said, there is something. It's actually rather time sensitive," Soames said, "we have a plane waiting for us, to take us back to London."

HUNT GAVE A LONG, slow whistle as they boarded the private jet. Soames flapped his tie and let it drop on his belly and pushed himself back into the white leather seats. Stirling took a seat opposite him.

"Is this the agency's?" Hunt asked and motioned to the luxury surroundings.

Soames shook his head, "No, belongs to Vail Corp. The Clubhouse is leasing it from them under the guise of an offshore registered company, and they are assisting us with the mission. Keep that in that quiet, off the books, untraceable space of civilian contracts and unoffialdom,"

Hunt didn't recognise the name.

"Huge mining conglomerate," Soames said, "they're assisting us with the mission."

"What mission?" Hunt asked.

A stewardess came up to the table and bent forward and held out a silver tray with two flutes of honey-coloured champagne. Hunt looked at Soames and waited to see if he would take one. He did and nodded 'thank you'. Stirling took his and had a small sip. The bubbles were sharp and prickly. She smiled and walked off and Hunt's eyes followed her. She moved like she knew he was looking.

Stirling picked up his glass, "Thanks Gerry, I don't know what would have happened if ..."

They clinked glasses. Soames took a sip.

"Don't mention it," he said, "but now, I have a favour to ask you in return."

Soames put his glass down and checked over his shoulder to make sure no-one was in earshot.

"Have you heard of McArthur Gentry?" he asked.

"Yes," Hunt said, "he's the fanatical human-butcher, and self-proclaimed holy man in charge of the Lord's Revelation Front."

"That's right. And now, he is also the proud keeper of Lord Langdon, codename Scratcher, the Prime Minister's son."

"He's been kidnapped?"

"Yes. And we have been tasked to get him back. This is a mission of the utmost secrecy, Stirling, we have a lot riding on finding him, before the news gets out. Vail have agreed to help the Government's effort to get Scratcher back, before there is a war."

Soames put his fingers on the base of his Champagne flute as the plane taxied down the runway.

"A war?"

"This is top secret, Hunt."

The aircraft built up speed down the runway now and Soames put his head back and looked out the window. The vibrations and shaking hit their peak and the swift lightness came over them and they were airborne. Soames put his head forward.

"It's strictly 'need to know' right now. We want to get him back before anyone else finds out, especially his mother."

"You mean the Prime Minister!" Hunt scoffed.

"Yes. I imagine that when his mother finds out that he is missing - possibly dead - at the hands of a terrorist. It has the potential to escalate very quickly."

Stirling watched Soames face. Soames looked tired, with bags under his eyes and a red-veiny nose.

"What is going on Gerry?"

"Money, son, money. And power. This is a struggle for power at the very top. And a lot of lives depend on the outcome. If we do our job right, we can have a profound influence on how this global game plays out. They have discovered vast amounts of platinum and God-knows-what else in Equatorial Varrissa and they want it. That is what it boils down to. But we need to make sure we can contain it as only that. We don't want to start a war."

"I don't know, Gerry. I am not involved in this anymore. I was out ..."

Soames furrowed his eyebrows.

"You didn't seem too out of it to me. And the Russians and the Chechens don't care if you are in or out. You need me, Hunt. You need *us*."

Stirling shook his head and took a sip of his champagne and the stewardess came past to offer them warm towels.

"Look, just remember I took a chance on you too, Hunt. There weren't exactly a lot of people at the Clubhouse clamouring for an untested, lame war hero to join up. I am giving you a chance. Where were you before? Injured, tossed on the scrap heap, but I saw something in you. And you proved me right. Whatever it is, you can't run forever. Sometimes you just have to stand and fight."

Stirling smiled at him. Soames' cheeks were flushed.

Soames saw Stirling grinning and his face relaxed. He picked up his glass and grinned at himself and took a sip.

"Why don't you just tell me what the mission is?"

"Okay," Soames said and set his glass down, "Find McArthur Gentry and eliminate him. Free hostages. Bring them back to the United Kingdom and avert a war. Easy peasy."

"Hostages? I thought you said it was only Lord Langdon."

Soames was quiet for a moment and studied Hunt's face.

"No. Your friend, Digger Gibson, is with them too."

Hunt's face hardened and his jaw clenched.

"Listen," Soames said and sensed his chance, "I'll make you a deal. Help me with this, get Langdon and Digger back, and I will help you with whatever you were looking for in Hungary, with whatever it is Kabazanov told you. How about it?"

Stirling eyed him up for a moment and Soames filled the gap.

"Damn it Hunt, you need to take a good hard look at yourself. This is your chance to make a difference, a real difference. To make something of yourself. You've got a skillset we need, and I know you want to use it."

"Alright, alright. Damn it Gerry," he said with a laugh, "you've made your point. I'll take a look at the operation. I'm not making any promises. I need to see what the risks are first, Digger knew what he was getting himself into."

Hunt swallowed hard after saying the last sentence. He knew he didn't sound convincing. And that wasn't how he felt, but he could see that Soames wasn't happy with his answer.

He also felt, maybe, it was enough for now.

"So why me, Gerry? Surely you have dozens of operatives ready for this?" Hunt asked.

Soames turned and looked at him. His face softened, but Stirling stiffened, prepared for a lie.

"You know, you have this peculiar, deep way of looking at people, Hunt. Like you're reading their faces for a clue. Like you're playing poker."

Hunt said nothing. His first thought was, this is a much more dangerous game than poker, for much higher stakes. His next was, you can tell a lot about the difference between what people say, and what the mean, by watching their reactions.

"Anyway, you hold your cards pretty close to your chest for a poker player, Hunt. We ran the mission details through the computer. You were one of three names it spat out. One of them was dead, the other one is injured, training recruits and consulting for the Navy. You're the only one capable of pulling this off," Soames said.

Hunt thought for a moment.

"There is another reason," Soames said as if it just occurred to him, "the Intelligence Director asked for you by name. Well, by codename."

Hunt looked quickly at Soames. He sat up, his body language showed he was interested. Soames looked surprised. Stirling realised he had intrigue written on his face, and then tried to seem nonchalant.

"You see," Soames said, "I told you, you always have a mischievous look on your face, Hunt. What is it about?"

Hunt shook his head.

"Well, first that I have a codename, you never told me."

"Ag, yes, well, I thought it fit nicely: Boatman. Because of you -"

"Nice. I get it," Hunt smiled, "but, didn't it make you wonder *why*? Why did the Director ask for me by name?"

"I don't know," Soames said, "because of your friendship with Digger, I presume."

Soames looked out the window in thought. Hunt didn't press the issue, but something nagged him inside. It didn't quite seem to add up. Soames slid out of his seat and stood up. He pulled a battered brown leather briefcase from the locker.

"Here," Soames said, and pulled out a file. He dropped it on the table with a *thud*.

"You can read all about Varrissa – and Gentry – in the report. That should help you make up your mind. And I need to know what it is by the time we land."

Hunt eyed up the grey folder and spun it with his index finger. He stared at the edge as his mind worked and he pursed his lips. He could feel Soames gaze as he looked down at him.

"Could this jet take us anywhere we want to go?" Hunt asked.

Soames stared at him blankly for a moment and then said cautiously, "Yes, I suppose so."

"Okay. Tell the pilot to change course. The only way we get this mission done is if I have something with me."

"Well, go on, tell me – what is it?"

"You'll see," Hunt said, "tell him to take us here," and scratched a name onto a bit of paper.

He handed it to Soames and he lifted his eyebrows as he read.

CHAPTER FOUR

ANGOLA, AFRICA

Hunt pushed the door open and walked into the bar and Soames followed. The sunlight outside dazzled and it took a moment for their eyes to adjust to the smokey gloom. The place was dark and smelled damp. Tinny African jazz played at low volume. It was a long room in the shape of a rectangle. There were booths to their right-hand side and a bar to their front. It looked like there were pool or snooker tables in the back. A lone figure was slumped on a stool at the bar. He was thick around the midriff. The barman appeared around the side and dried a glass with a stained dishcloth.

"Come on," Hunt said over his shoulder.

He walked up and put both hands on the bar and looked dead ahead. The figure next to him didn't move. The figure was looking at his glass and then lifted a tumbler to his lips and took a sip and cleared his throat.

"I was wondering when you'd come. If you're here for the diamond money, I don't have it."

"I thought I might find you here," Hunt said.

VD harrumphed.

"*Ja*, well ..."

"I'm not here about the diamond. In fact, let's not mention it right now. I brought someone I'd like you to meet," Hunt said.

VD turned to look at Hunt and a smile broke out across his face.

"You're looking a bit worse than the last time I saw you," VD said.

He was enthused.

"You're looking a hell of a lot better than the last time I saw you," Hunt said.

VD's face dropped slightly and he took a sip of his brandy, "cheers to that," he said, "what happened to your pretty face?"

Hunt didn't answer and indicated Soames and VD spun on the stool to see. Soames walked forward and put out his hand, VD took it firmly and looked at Hunt, curious.

"Gerry Soames, this is Johan van Driebek."

"How do you do," Soames said.

"Let's go to a booth?" Hunt suggested and looked at the bartender.

They squeezed into the leather seats. VD sat opposite Hunt and Soames.

"Good to see you old pal," Hunt said, "VD was with me in Zimbabwe," he clarified for Soames' benefit, and Soames nodded.

VD was more haggard and husky than usual. His beard was long and fanned out. His bush hat sat low on his brow and he perspired through his khaki shirt.

Hunt watched him closely.

"Don't give me that look," VD said from under his hat

and Hunt shrugged. VD pulled an envelope of tobacco and papers out and put them on the table.

"So, what's this all about?" he asked and rolled a cigarette.

"Where's your pipe?" Hunt asked.

"They don't like me smoking it in here, but they don't mind the cigarettes as much," VD said.

"This is highly sensitive information ..." Soames said urgently.

Hunt raised a hand to calm him, like he was slowing down a taxi.

"I trust this man with my life," he said, "he's okay."

Hunt could see VD was intrigued as he licked along the edge of the roll-up and tapped it on his lighter. Soames fanned himself with his Panama hat and dabbed his forehead.

"It's a bit complicated to explain VD, but what do you know about Equatorial Varrissa?" Hunt asked.

VD flicked his Zippo lighter closed and took a drag of the cigarette. The smoke rose around his beard and under the peak of his hat and he inhaled sharply, shook his head, and tapped the ash.

"I was with Executive Outcomes in Sierra Leone during the civil war, and I hear that was like a stroll through the gardens in comparison with Varrissa," VD said and wiped a bit of tobacco from his tongue.

"Each strongman dictator has been worse than the previous one. Paranoid, psychotic. They all look like ratty accountants. Public executions are commonplace. Ritualistic beatings and intimidation by the Secret Police. Something like three-hundred thousand prisoners in Black Beach prison, out of a population of about a million and a half, and then ten or twenty-thousand of those prisoners are found guilty of treason and executed on a regular basis; and somehow they are almost always political opponents."

VD looked at Hunt and Soames in turn and tapped the ash.

"Why do you ask?"

Hunt looked at Soames, and Soames gave a single, solemn nod.

"We're planning a top secret operation, and could really use your help."

VD scoffed and took a drag.

"What's it this time, another diamond smuggling operation?" VD narrowed his eyes and exhaled the smoke.

"Not quite," Hunt said, "It's a bit more complicated. More of a rescue mission. But we need someone with your skill set, and who knows their way around Africa and the bush. We could use someone like you."

"Who is *we*?"

"Officially a mining exploration company called Earth-eye."

"And unofficially?"

Soames raised his hand this time, "the British Intelligence Service, Mister van Driebek. A high-value target has been kidnapped by McArthur Gentry, and we need him back."

"McArthur Gentry," VD repeated softly and stubbed his cigarette out, "you have to be kidding. I am not going anywhere near that madman," he said as he edged out of the booth. He'd heard enough.

Hunt looked at Soames who shrugged, and grabbed VD by the wrist.

"No, no, no, I am not interested, *at all*," VD shook his head, "and neither should you be, Stirling," he said and looked down at him.

He pulled his arm away and Hunt let it go. VD straightened himself.

"If your hostages are even alive," VD said and pulled on the front of his shirt to unstick it, "Gentry is holed up in the one contested part of the country that President Debby can't get a foothold in. It's a free-for-all, basically impenetrable bush, doubtful if we would ever even find him, and if we do, what then? He's been known to eat people, you know?"

VD walked to the bar and called out to the bartender.

"Give me a second," Hunt said to Soames.

He went and leaned his elbows on the bar.

"Been back here long?" Hunt asked.

"*Ag*, off and on," VD said and took a sip of his drink. "You some sort of special agent now?" and scoffed.

"I haven't decided to take the job yet."

"Oh *ja*, why not?"

"I need you, partner."

VD grunted and dismissed the comment with a wave of his hand and looked away.

"Look, I know I owe you one," VD said and turned and looked at Hunt's face, "but this mission is suicide."

"That's why I need you."

VD shook his head.

"You don't owe me," Hunt said, "you never have. If anything I owe you ... but, one of the hostages is one of the blokes, you know, a guy I went through basic with and who always had my back. I know he wouldn't leave me there if he could do something about it. I know that doesn't mean much to you, because you don't know him, but that is why I need to go. But, I also need someone to watch my back, mate. Plus, they'll pay."

VD's eyes glinted and his ears pricked up. He tried to suppress the smile and sipped his drink. *Same old VD*, Hunt thought. He gave VD an open-palmed pat on the shoulder and they laughed.

"Well, why didn't you say so!?" he joked and the barman smiled as he twisted glass in a cloth.

"How much?" VD asked.

Hunt shrugged, "you name it, Her Majesty is picking up the tab."

VD sat back and looked at the ceiling. Hunt could see he

was playing with the idea. Hunt could see him thinking about toying with the bait.

"Listen," Hunt said and pulled some change from his pocket and put it on the bar. He slid a seven-sided silver fifty-pence coin and placed it on his thumb, "I'm not sure about this mission either, but you know I like the concept of winner take all. If you win, stay here if you want to. If not, you come to London and at least listen to the plan. Call it in the air?"

VD watched and Hunt flicked the coin, it looped up, he caught it and slapped it down on the back of his hand. Hunt looked into his friend's eyes.

"Heads," VD said.

REPUBLIC OF EQUATORIAL VARRISSA, WEST AFRICA

DIGGER HAD CAUGHT glimpses of the glistening summit as the vehicles bounced and spun their wheels up the mud roads, before they were forced out of the vehicles to march the rest of the way. They were deep in the jungle, somewhere to the north-west of Mount Lamia.

Lord Langdon, Simeone and himself had been frisked and his mobile phone, watch, belt and shoes were removed, before they were made to march into the ominous thick green of the forest.

There was a single trail running into the jungle and Gentry's soldiers were meticulous about camouflaging the vehicles and replacing bent or damaged foliage to cover their tracks. They marched at a steady pace for a day and spent one night out in the open at the mercy of mosquitoes and insects, before arriving at Gentry's lair the next morning.

At first, it wasn't clear if they'd arrived in the camp. There was a circular clearing and the ground was redder and drier than the carpet of leaves and mud under the trees. They were forced into the bush on a path that ran from the clearing and Digger noticed low-slung, thatched roofs of huts with open walls. The open-walled huts reminded him of a thatch gazebo.

The soldiers guarding the three of them stank and pushed them with the butts of their rifles into the hut. It was dark under the roof. They'd been forced to climb into a straw lined wooden cage set against the back of a rock wall. It was damp and covered with moss.

Water trickled down the face and followed a path down the slope away from their cell. The ground and straw was damp. Digger had no doubt that they were prisoners now, for how long, he had no idea.

A single guard was left to watch over them. This one was young, maybe sixteen, Digger thought. And he watched them with thin, deep set eyes sunk into high, chubby cheekbones. He sat on a plastic container with his rifle in one hand, and drew with a stick in the dirt with the other, and looked up and caught their eyes as he did. Digger could hear the sounds of other soldiers as they moved in the forest around them, but the hut's roof was slung low and he couldn't see out.

Lord Langdon elbowed Digger gently in the knee.

"Where's your mobile phone?" Langdon whispered.

Digger shook his head, "they took it."

"Damn it."

"Yours?"

"Still in the aircraft."

"It was no use," Digger said, "mine lost signal before we disembarked the vehicles."

"They're going to kill us," Simeone whimpered.

The three prisoners were seated with their backs against

36

the cold rock wall and the cage was just big enough for them to sit with their knees pulled up against their chins.

"They aren't going to kill us," Digger said, "not yet, anyway."

"They're cannibals," Simeone said and looked across at Digger and Langdon.

A shout came from the young guard, "Shut up!"

Simeone put his face down between his knees and sobbed.

"Just don't piss yourself," Digger said to him out the side of his mouth.

The guard stood up and threw his drawing stick down. He ducked under the thatched roof and stuck the rifle barrel between the slats of the cage.

"Stop talking, now, or I punish you. Hear?" he said slow and soft, which gave it more menace.

Langdon put up his palms in surrender and nodded. The guard turned his back to leave.

"Where are we?" Langdon asked as the guard went back to his plastic drum seat.

"Somewhere north of the mountain," Digger said, "but I lost sight of it through the thickness."

Digger smacked his neck, "poxy malaria merchant," he growled.

The heat and humidity was stifling and they all sweated, sitting cramped in their cage. Digger's throat was dry.

"Water. Water, please," Lord Langdon said to the guard.

The guard sucked his tooth and slowly stood. He started to wander off and then saw another soldier. He shouted something to him and came back and sat down and drew in the soil with his stick. They heard more talking. The guard's colleague had come back. The colleague ducked under the roof and walked up to the bars and grinned like a mongoloid. He taunted them like they were monkeys in a zoo. He dipped his hand in the white plastic bucket and flicked water at them. Simeone tried to catch some and scrambled on top of Langdon.

"Settle down, Simeone. For God's sake," Langdon said.

The taunter's face dropped and he took a step back.

"You've taken the Lord's name in vain," he mumbled.

"I, I'm terribly sorry," Langdon said, "I didn't mean to."

The taunter didn't seem impressed by this. He set the bucket down and turned to leave and then changed his mind. He looked at the three of them sitting hunched in the wooden cage. He walked back to the bucket.

"Thank you, thank you -" Langdon said.

The taunter put his foot on the bucket and pushed it over with his foot.

"No, no, no ..." the water spilled out onto the mud. He laughed again and left and the three men were forced to scoop what they could from the sand. Simeone twisted his neck to lick the water on the rock face.

As it grew darker the noise from the forest increased, like someone turned up the volume on a stereo. Animals screeched and screamed in the trees. A choir of crickets chirruped all around them.

They were left alone. They hadn't eaten. The men put their heads between their legs and tried to sleep. Before they did, in the quiet moment of contemplation, Langdon looked at Digger in the darkness.

"What do you think happened to all of our boys?" Lord Langdon asked.

"I don't know, boss. I saw a lot of bodies at the ambush site. I think we have to assume if they aren't here with us, they are all dead."

"And the other group?"

Digger shook his head in the darkness.

"No idea. Compromised. Expect the worst, hope for the best?"

The canopy of trees around them completely covered the

sky. There was no ambient light. Digger couldn't see his hand in front of his face. He only heard the occasional slaps as Simeone and Langdon swatted at the mosquitoes as they attacked. He closed his eyes and tried to sleep.

———

DIGGER'S HEAD bobbed between his legs and he heard a faint rustling sound, and then hushed voices that grew louder the closer they came. He saw the swishing white light of head torches coming their way. The jungle seemed to grow quiet around them. The animals stopped and the crickets moved. There was only the noise of the voices. Digger elbowed Langdon in the ribs to wake him.

"Something's up," he said.

"Huh, what is it?"

"I don't know."

"Simeone. Simeone, wake up," Langdon said and the personal secretary lifted his head and rubbed his eyes. As he did the white light lit several pairs of feet as they ducked under the thatched roof.

"What's going on?" Langdon demanded.

They pulled open the cage and grabbed Simeone. He screamed and tried to fight them off. Langdon grabbed Simeone and fought to pull him in. There was a scuffle. One of the soldiers brought his rifle butt down on Langdon's cheek and he fell back and clutched his face.

"No! Help me! Help me, please!" Simeone screamed as they dragged him away. The lights and feet disappeared.

"Don't get in our way," the last man said as he locked them in again.

"Bastards," Langdon said after they left. He held his fingers out and tried to see the blood.

The crickets started up again and soon the whole choir was back at full pelt. Other animals screeched and croaked and knocked in the forest around them. After some time they heard a different sound. They both held their breath.

"Do you hear that?" Digger whispered.

"Shh, shh, listen," Langdon said.

They looked at each other in the dark. It was a scream. Then silence. And then a high pitched, terrified scream again.

"No. My God," Langdon said and lifted his hands to his face.

"They're torturing the poor bastard," Digger said and swallowed hard. *Maybe we're next*, he thought.

"Listen, Digger," Langdon said and put his hand on Digger's knee, "if anything should happen to me -"

"We don't need to worry about that yet boss. Let's not even think it. We're going to get out of here. Someone will come."

"Who the hell are they going to send? How the hell are they even going to know where we are in this godforsaken place?"

Simeone's scream rang out and birds in the trees took flight. It was a horrible sound. Digger covered his ears. When he looked up again there were two men standing in front of the cage.

"You're coming with us," one said, as the other showed them his rifle and pointed it at them. "Come. Out. Now," he barked.

They climbed out of the narrow gate, their bodies were cramped and sore, they'd been sitting like that for hours. Langdon groaned and stretched his back.

"Move," the one with the rifle said and pushed Langdon with the butt.

It was dark and Digger had a hard time following the one in front. The soldier moved smoothly and confidently through the foliage. Langdon put his hand on Digger's shoulder and followed close behind and stumbled through the bush and vines. After some time walking the ground seemed to slope away. They were following a rocky trail. It went downhill and into a kind of pit, or valley. And then Digger saw the light of a fire. It flickered against the stone walls around them. He heard people in the distance. When they came upon the scene Digger saw Gentry sitting at the head of a long stone table. It looked like it was carved out of the surrounding rock. The fire flickered and jigged off ornately carved figurines and faces carved into the walls. There were men sitting in the shadows all around them.

When Gentry saw them he called and waved them over, "My guests! Welcome. Please join me."

The one with the rifle jabbed Digger in the back and pushed him forward. As they walked up they saw the fire, and behind it, Simeone. He hung naked from a meat hook and dangled over a wooden pyre. His feet and mouth were bound. There was a group of soldiers standing around him with bloody clothes and bloody hands. One of them held his cigarette onto Simeone's skin and he screamed through the cloth over his mouth and writhed.

"Please, sit," Gentry said again.

Langdon moved to sit on a stone pew.

"Not! There …" Gentry said fiercely, "you will sit here," he pointed to the ground near his feet, "like the dogs you are."

They sat down on the ground.

"Why are you torturing him?" Langdon demanded.

Gentry looked over at Simeone as he dangled in the fire's light. The blood on him glistened.

"Because, I am not satisfied with his confession."

"How can he bloody confess when he has a rag stuffed down his throat?" Langdon protested and almost got up. Digger put his hand on Langdon's shoulder. Langdon glanced at him and Digger shook his head. Gentry laughed and popped some meat into his mouth and chewed loudly.

"He has also offended the god," Gentry said.

"Offended God, how has he offended God!?" Langdon cried.

"Not, 'God'," Gentry said and pointed to the stars. He leaned down and said softly, "the god of this place, the god in these walls," and sat up and went back to chewing.

The soldiers took turns beating Simeone's body and he wailed and coughed as the air was knocked out of him. Langdon was quiet now, the anger had run out of him and he sat deflated on the ground. Gentry tossed him a piece of meat and it landed in the dirt.

"Eat," he said.

Langdon just looked away.

"What do you want with us?" Langdon said quietly.

"Nothing," Gentry said and sucked meat from between his teeth and wiped his hand down the front of his shirt, "you're here to watch the sacrifice."

Gentry stood and shouted, "bring him."

The group in front of Simeone looked at one another and then got together to lift him off the hook. They carried him between them. Digger could see his chest rising and falling and his face was swollen with blood from being upside down. His eyes nearly closed due to the punches. Gentry walked around the side of the table and the soldiers placed Simeone's body face down with his torso and head on the table.

Gentry looked at Langdon as he spoke, "I wondered for the longest time about this line in this table," he said and ran his finger down a groove carved into the middle of it.

"Then one day, I spilled my wine, and it ran into the groove. And I realised this table was tilted away from where the boy is now," he pointed at Simeone with a blade that glinted in the light. "I began to realise that this, all around us, was a temple. There is a god here. Not the Lord Almighty, but a spirit, some being. And I knew it must not be displeased with me. I studied the ruins. I read the carvings in the walls and God spoke to me and told me what I must do.

He said, "'McArthur, you are my servant. You must make a sacrifice to keep this spirit happy. If you do, you will be rich. You will be able to win the Presidency of this Republic.' That is what God told me in my dream."

Langdon couldn't watch. Gentry pointed the blade at Simeone who breathed hard through his nose and glared wide-eyed and in terror at the man to his front. Gentry walked up behind Simeone where the soldiers were holding him. He grabbed the back of his his hair and yanked his head back to expose his neck, like you would with a pig. One of the soldiers removed the binding from his mouth and Simeone screamed.

Gentry closed his eyes and said in a low hum, "I will extol the Lord at all times; His praise will always be on my lips. I will glorify myself in the Lord; let the afflicted hear and rejoice. Glorify the Lord with me; let us exalt his name together."

Simeone screamed and Gentry yanked the blade across his neck and drove it in deep. The crunch and slicing sound made Digger gag. Simeone's scream turned into a gurgle. His eyes bulged in his head and his body thrashed. Gentry turned his face away as the blood sprayed from his artery and then twisted his head. Digger could look at nothing, but the blood channel carved into the table. Like lava, viscous and congealed, it ran into the channel and turned the white stone crimson. It ran, gentle at first, and then gathered speed down the table, like a wave in a river. The body went limp and Gentry walked around to the other side and met the first drops of human blood as it dripped off the table. He held a wooden bowl underneath with both hands and collected it, like he was asking for another bowl of soup.

Digger's mind recoiled at the horror of the spectacle. He felt like he floated. Like in a dream. He watched himself watching the events unfold. Men climbed out of shadows and caves in the rock walls around them, they filed in, like boarding school boys for afternoon tea. Digger watched, but his mind wasn't there. They flayed the body and stripped the skin. They cut off the head and left it on the table. The bulging grotesque eyes watched them as they hung the body back above the flames and cooked it. The heavy air filled with the tang scent of roasting meat. And all Digger could hear was the crackle and spits, like a Sunday joint.

CHAPTER FIVE

LONDON, UNITED KINGDOM

"Listen we're simply behind the curve on this one," Hunt heard as he stepped up to the opening of the glass sliding door.

He tapped on the glass and pulled it wider. The branding on the wall above a monitor said, 'Earth-eye'. All the people in the meeting turned to look at him and he gave a quick, polite smile. The man who'd spoken the words was standing at the head of a conference table with his sleeves rolled loosely up, and with his hands on his hips. He watched Hunt and raised his eyebrows questioningly.

"I'm Stirling, I believe you're expecting me?"

"Ah," the man said, "Yes. Everyone, this is Stirling Hunt."

Hunt looked at each of the people at the table in turn. A few nodded hello. A few looked back at the guy standing at the front.

"Come in please," he said and gestured to a black leather

chair at the back of the table, "I am Trevor Watkins, Head of Operations at Earth-eye."

Hunt nodded hello and lifted his hand and gave a wave to the faces that looked back at him.

"We'll get to introductions in a minute," Trevor said, "but for now let's all get on the same page. As I was saying, we need to be in Equatorial Varrissa within seventy-two hours."

There was a stillness after the announcement. A man in thick spectacles to Hunt's left dropped his head and shook it.

"I know it is going to be tight," Trevor said, "but we have to get this done. Alright? President Debby has made the discovery of mineral rights a competition and the prize for finding the most lucrative deposits are mining rights in perpetuity. The European and Chinese teams are already in the country. So we need to be faster and smarter."

Hunt knew that Trevor was referring to the current president of Equatorial Varrissa, the maniacal dictator, Debby Mabosongo. One of the longest serving dictators in Africa, he'd taken power from his uncle in a violent and bloody coup d'etat and held onto it with a reign defined by fear and terror. It was said that he personally attended the brutal torture and interrogation sessions. They still had ritual public executions in front of the cheering throngs. Hacked to death by *panga* was said to be his favourite.

The thick-spectacled man raised his hand and then let it drop back to the table. "It simply can't be done, Trevor, we don't have the resources available," he said.

Trevor glanced at Stirling and said, "Cameron. Logistics."

Cameron looked at Stirling and gave him a polite half-smile.

"We'll have to repurpose the Nepal expedition," Trevor said.

Cameron pushed his spectacles up the bridge of his nose and the woman in a white lab coat to Trevor's left objected with an open mouth.

"That is my expedition Trevor, you promised I would be taking the next one. We've been planning it for months," the woman in the lab coat said.

Trevor looked at Hunt again and was about to speak, but he was cut off. The auburn haired woman in the lab coat turned and said, "Matilda Chasm, Project Leader, everyone calls me Maddy."

Stirling watched her as she made her case to the Head of Operations. She was fair skinned and pale. Too much sitting indoors looking at computer monitors, he guessed. Her fingernails were short and manicured and Hunt noticed the engagement ring on her slender finger. He thought she looked a bit young to be a project leader.

"Let's talk about this afterwards," Trevor said firmly and she gritted her teeth and looked down at her notepad. She glanced up at Hunt and he looked away. *Busted*, he thought and tried not to smile. He could feel her eyes piercing the side of his face.

"Okay," Trevor said, "Let's go around the room," and gestured to a dark skinned man to his right. The man gave Stirling a big smile. He had a large head and big hands and he lifted a cream-coloured palm up.

"Hello, I am Timothy Fabrice from Cameroon. I am an Earth-eye linguistic expert, with a focus on west Africa."

"Thanks, next," Trevor indicated the next man.

"Hi, I am Delvin Arden," he swept his brown hair to the side, "I am project technician and signals engineer, planned to go to Nepal with Maddy here," he said and lifted a finger towards her, "and by the way, I was in the Special Air Service, so if you ever need someone to show you the ropes, let me know. Happy to help."

"Thanks, I'll be sure to remember that," Hunt said and thought it was an odd thing to mention straight away and out of the blue.

Cameron, the spectacled man, looked at Stirling and pushed them up his nose again.

"Cameron," he said, "I work in operations and logistics for Trevor. I make sure everything is arranged before you travel."

They all turned to look at Hunt expectantly.

"Ah, Hunt. Stirling Hunt. I've been brought in due to the political situation in country. I have experience of mining operations in Africa and look forward to getting to know you all a lot better."

Trevor nodded, "Stirling is Vail's man on this expedition. We know it is a race against the Germans and the Chinese and the Russians and he is here to help us win this thing," they all turned back to Trevor.

There was one person who hadn't introduced himself. He was an old man in a tartan sports jacket and wore a black beret. He sat on Stirling's right. Trevor saw Hunt looking at the old man. The old man ignored him.

"Stirling, this is Colonel Jack Mulrooney, he's our external consultant on African expeditions."

Hunt had heard of him. He was known as 'Mad Jack', an infamous mercenary and one of the figures that emerged during the rise of African independence, first in the Congo and then later in Varrissa. He'd been sentenced to twenty years imprisonment in Black Beach prison.

He gave a grunt.

"That makes me think," Trevor said, "We are missing someone for this expedition. We still need a local guide, someone who knows the area, the locals, and can arrange the logistics on the ground."

Cameron rubbed his chin, "maybe du Toit?" he suggested.

Trevor shook his head, "No, he has been approached by the Russian consortium."

"I think I have the perfect replacement," Hunt said.

On cue there was a commotion in the hallway. The sliding glass door to the conference room *swooshed* open and Trevor's

Executive Assistant stepped in. She was clipped and professional in her movements. Everyone turned to look. Hunt turned slowly and followed their gaze.

The assistant beckoned with her hand and VD stepped into the meeting room looking at the woman. He was still in his bush hat, mid-thigh khaki shorts and socks rolled over the laces of his brown leather boots. He turned slowly and took a slight step back when he saw the room silent and watching him. Hunt gave him a broad grin and pulled out a chair for him. VD came over and took a seat next to Hunt.

As he sat he leaned over and said, "You never bloody told me it was a Ging Gang Goolie."

Maddy made a noise that sounded like a laugh and bit down on her pen and smiled. Trevor raised his eyebrows and looked at Hunt with expectation on his face.

"This is my friend and the missing member of our team, if you don't mind me saying, Johan van Driebek. Call him VD. He's our expert on Africa," Hunt said and gave VD a pat on the shoulder.

"Hello," VD said simply with a small wave of the hand.

"Well, you certainly look the part," Trevor said. "Welcome."

VD nodded.

The large African man in a bright white shirt to VD's left put out his hand. It was elongated with neatly manicured fingers. He said, "Hello, I am Timothy Fabrice. I'm the team's linguist."

"Nice to meet you," VD said and shook it firmly.

Fabrice sat back and interlaced his hands on his flat stomach and leaned back.

"And so, that is the expedition team then," Trevor said.

They all looked around at each other. It felt like an uneasy truce.

"Except for the man on the ground, someone mentioned

du Toit?" Trevor asked rhetorically, "The Varrissa government hate du Toit."

"So what?" Mad Jack spat and nearly lost his dentures, "he's bloody resourceful, and he knows the area better than anyone. Trained him myself," he said.

Cameron tapped his pen on the table, "just so I am clear, and because I am arranging the diplomatic side of things, are we proposing essentially entering a sovereign state illegally and led by a former mercenary soldier?"

VD looked at Hunt.

"Um, almost half of us around this table are mercenary soldiers," Hunt said and Mad Jack threw his head back and laughed. Trevor smiled.

"Not at all, Cameron, we will of course go through the official channels, but I want to hire the best men for the job," Trevor said with a subtle nod to Hunt and VD. "Anything else?"

"There is just one other problem," the logistics man, Cameron, said, "the Nepal trip is a mountain expedition," he waved the end of his pen as he spoke.

"You can modify the units in nine hours," Trevor said and looked around the room. "Anything else?"

No-one spoke.

"We have leased a cargo jet that will be arriving at Heathrow in nine hours. So that is your window to prep the kit. Visas are in progress and will need to be stamped on arrival in Varrissa. We have one shot at this. I have it on good authority that there is a delegation from the Chinese consortium spending Yuan in Puerto-Nuevo by the bucket load."

"Yes," Mad Jack said with effort and looked at the people around the table in turn, "you need whiskey, crates of the stuff, cheap shoes and disposable cameras."

"What for?" Cameron asked.

"Why, bribes of course!" Mad Jack said.

Cameron laughed, thinking he was joking. The old colonel

lifted a gnarled forefinger and held it out, "Listen, sonny boy, I was planning raids in Africa since before you were a twinkle in your father's eye, and I was taking shrapnel in Nigeria, when you were still shitting in a nappy and wiping it on your face, so don't tell me I don't understand."

Mad Jack looked over to VD, and VD nodded, "He's right. You should do what he says."

"So," Trevor interjected, "note that down please Cameron. Any particular brand of Scotch or ... ?" he asked and looked at Mad Jack. The old colonel threw his head back and laughed. It broke the tension and they all joined in. Fabrice boomed. Only Delvin didn't seem to laugh.

VD caught Hunt's eye while everyone chuckled and raised his eyebrows. *VD wasn't feeling confident*, Hunt thought. Everyone settled down. VD cleared his throat and pointed to the map on the screen behind Trevor, who turned to look at it.

Equatorial Varrissa was a half-moon shaped country nestled into the shoulder of west Africa. Curved around it, like a rainbow, was an independent country called the Côte d'Ambre. It surrounded Varrissa on all sides. The map was topographical and brightly coloured. The orange and green colours of the inland highlands running down to the dense green towards the coast. Two major rivers flowed north-east to south-west and ran parallel to one another. They bisected the country into thirds and both bulged near the top of the map as they flowed wide around the country's highest peak, Mount Lamia. That was the new post-colonial name, the British had called it the Emerald Mountain, or the Glass Mountain, on account of the glistening and shimmering mist from the waterfalls that streaked down its sides and caught the light of the sun. The peak was a white blot on the map, indicating its height, and it dominated the geography inland.

"I have a question," VD said, "where exactly are we going to look for minerals in this country?"

Trevor cleared his throat and picked up a laser pointer. He shone the red dot on the screen and held it to the north-east of Mount Lamia.

"Our earth resourcing satellite imaging and analysis of the geology indicate our best chance of success is starting in this area stretching from the north-east base of the mountain out for several kilometres."

VD nodded, "*Ja*, that is what I was worried about. You know that area is a conflict zone, right? Debby's troops don't control it."

Trevor put the pointer down, "We know," he said quietly.

"Okay," VD said, "and how exactly do you plan on getting there?"

"Drive from Puerto-Nuevo," Delvin said simply.

VD sat back in the leather chair and rubbed his chin. He caught Hunt's eye and shook his head almost imperceptibly, so only Hunt could see.

"How far is that drive?" Hunt asked.

"About six-hundred miles," Trevor said, and waved his hand at the map.

"Off-road through barely navigable terrain with two vehicles and kit," Hunt said. He made it sound like a question, but his tone was incredulous.

"That's right," Delvin the communications guy said, "is there a problem with that?"

Hunt eyed him up. Delvin sounded defensive about the challenge to the infiltration method.

"And how long would that take?" Hunt asked the group, and watched Delvin out the corner of his eye.

Cameron sucked his cheek and punched numbers into a calculator and scratched sums on a pad in front of him. He wobbled his head from side to side, "around twelve hours, I should think, everything being equal."

"So twelve hours, assuming no issues on the road," Hunt said.

Cameron nodded.

"There is no other way," Delvin said.

"Unless there is," VD shot back and glared at him.

"Well, let's hear it," Trevor said and held his palms up to call Delvin off his attack.

The others watched as Hunt stood and made his way round the table to the screen.

"We fly into Puerto-Nuevo," Hunt pointed to the coastal city in the south-west of the country, "we have to clear customs."

The others nodded.

"Instead of sourcing Land Rovers and relying on local fixers, what if we load up into another aircraft?"

"And land where?" Delvin scoffed, "there is nothing but rainforest for a thousand miles in all directions."

Hunt traced his hand along a flight path, over the Emerald Mountain, over the border into the surrounding country of Côte d'Ambre, "Here," he said and stabbed his index finger into the screen, "Kissidou Airport in the Amber Coast."

"That's not even the right country!" Delvin cried out and dropped his pen on the table.

"Hold on," Trevor said to him, "hear him out. What's the plan, Hunt?"

"It's a bush runway," Hunt said, "but the Rio Moa river runs past it directly to the east, and, if you trace the river down into Equatorial Varrissa ..."

"It horseshoes around Mount Lamia to the west," Trevor finished his sentence.

"We'd save twenty-four hours," Hunt said, "and, we'd have an extraction point a few hundred miles north-west of our area of operations. We wouldn't be reliant on vehicles and a six-hundred mile journey on mud roads if something goes wrong."

"And what, clear immigration in the Côte d'Ambre *again*," Delvin said.

"No you *pillock*," Mad Jack spat at him, "that's why you've taken the whiskey!"

Cameron was scrawling notes on his pad, and Fabrice rubbed his chin and nodded along.

Fabrice pointed at the screen and said, "if we could get a flat bottomed Patrol Boat, we could navigate the Moa no matter the rainfall or depth situation."

Hunt nodded.

"And it's a great base of operations," VD said.

"Colonel, what do you think?" Trevor asked.

The old colonel looked at each of the crew in turn and then his eyes dropped and looked at his arthritic, knotted fingers.

"I wish to hell I was going with you," he said, "it's going to be a hell-of-an expedition."

"And about the plan with the boats?" Delvin said.

"I think you'd be idiotic to do anything else," Mad Jack said and held Delvin's gaze with ice-blue eyes. Delvin looked away and picked up his pen. Trevor watched him. Delvin glanced up and nodded.

"Okay," he said.

"Anybody else?" Trevor asked.

They shook their heads.

"So, that's it. Wheels up in nine hours, get a move on."

They all pushed the chairs back and stood up to leave.

"Hunt," Trevor said and Stirling turned, "can I see you in my office? Five minutes."

"Sure," he said, and saw Maddy watching him from the doorway.

"Down the hall on the right," Trevor said, "be there in a minute."

Hunt nodded and turned to go.

He walked out of the conference room, he felt a buzz of

excitement at the mission and VD was onboard. He turned right and checked the nameplates for Trevor's office.

He walked past one of the open doors and heard a voice.

"Make no mistake, Mister Hunt, I am in charge of this expedition."

He stopped and turned back.

Maddy Chasm stood in her lab coat just inside a darkened office with a notepad under her arm. She leaned on the back of a chair. Hunt stood in the doorway.

"I am in charge of this expedition," she repeated, this time to his face, "Not you. You're an unfortunate, necessary requirement. The only reason you're here is because of the state of insecurity in the country. You might have hijacked the infiltration plan, but this is not your operation, do you understand?"

Hunt nodded.

"I am in charge," she said again, "You're a bodyguard, nothing more. Do your job. Take care of your side of things and we won't have any problems. Got it?"

Hunt opened his mouth to reply and she pushed past him and dug her shoulder into his rib cage. He laughed, taken aback, and watched her shiny auburn hair bounce down the corridor.

"I saw you practicing that speech to yourself in the meeting!" he yelled after her.

She held her middle finger up over her shoulder and kept walking.

CHAPTER SIX

Hunt's meeting with Trevor was frank and direct. Trevor made it clear that the safety of his team was his top priority, "but we have a contractual obligation to Vail Corp and their backing is the only way we can keep this company's project going. Listen," Trevor said, "I know she might seem like a soft beauty with a seductive accent, but Maddy is tough, and she is very smart."

"Why've you put her in charge of this mission?" Hunt asked.

"She earned it," Trevor said, "she is very driven. If the mission goes wrong it is going to take someone strong enough to talk her out of it, so I thought I would give you a heads-up. She's highly intelligent and she is used to being smarter than most of the men, and she uses that to get what she wants."

"And she bullied you into letting her lead this mission, did she?" Hunt asked.

Trevor shook his head.

"Believe it or not, she actually is the best person for this one."

"And the others?"

"They're a good team," Trevor said, "Fabrice will know

about the tribes and their customs. If he doesn't know the local dialects, he will pick it up very fast. Delvin is ex-Forces, like you I assume, he is a technical guy. Don't let his attitude get you down, he means well."

Hunt rubbed his chin and stared at the desk.

"If you haven't decided if you're going on this operation yet," Trevor said, "I wanted to ask you to, because they're going to need someone like you ..." Hunt looked up, "what I mean to say is, Nigel Dodder spoke very highly of your experience in Africa. I think they are going to need it ... so, ah, what do you say? Welcome aboard?" Trevor stuck out his hand from across the desk and smiled awkwardly.

Hunt looked at it for a second and then said, "Screw it, we're in," and gripped his hand.

THE NEXT DAY VD and Hunt stood on the tarmac and watched as the gear for the expedition was loaded into an unmarked Boeing 747-200.

"We're never going to clear customs in Varrissa," VD said with a gruff and squeezed a glob of spit onto the tarmac.

Hunt took a step back and looked at him.

"Chewing tobacco," VD said, "the only way I am going to survive this bloody flight."

Cameron, the square-spectacled logistics man, walked up with his clipboard under his arm. He gave them a smile and took off his hardhat and rubbed his sweaty hair.

"What the hell are those?" Hunt asked and pointed to the plastic crates being loaded by conveyor through the gaped mouth of the aircrafts hinged nose. It looked like a basking shark feeding on plankton.

"Ah, those are our transport containers, all the gear for the expedition," Cameron said.

"A lot of stuff," VD said and looked sideways at him.

"That's not the half of it. Your river Patrol Boat is in pieces inside there too. Nifty bit of engineering if I do say so myself, but you'll have to assemble it on the other side," Cameron said and shook his head.

"What about our weapons?" Hunt asked.

"I nearly forgot," Cameron said and lifted a finger, "hold on a moment." He went over to a pile of kit, set off to the side.

"I put them in these," he said as he walked back. He held a long plastic black tele-tube by its nylon shoulder strap. Hunt took it from him. It was lightweight, but felt solid.

"Strong and light and easy to carry I figured," Cameron said and wiped the back of his hand across his sweaty brow. "Because, I have some bad news on the weapons."

VD turned to face him now and Cameron took a small step back and gave a nervous laugh.

"I tried to get the," he checked his clipboard, "Galil ACE 31s like you asked, but it was too short notice."

VD looked at Stirling quickly and back at Cameron. He didn't look happy with that news.

"I did manage to get two M4 Carbines and two M16 rifles. I figured you'd be able to get ammunition more easily for something like the M16, if you needed it. Everything else on the list I managed to procure. du Toit will have the Claymores ready for when you arrive."

Hunt put his hands over his face and shook his head. VD took his bush hat off and stepped forward. Cameron cowered and stepped back again. Hunt put his hand into VD's chest and pushed him back gently. He gave him a look that said 'calm down'.

"I am sorry. Have I done something wrong?" Cameron said. He looked pathetic.

"The only issue with the ammunition is, like most third world countries, they use Kalashnikov variants," Hunt said.

Cameron nodded without understanding and Hunt felt

his blood pressure rise and his frustration turned to anger. He turned away and bit down on his fist to stop himself exploding and then took a deep breath. He heard his heartbeat thumping in his ears.

"They use different calibre bullets," VD said with indignation and Hunt could hear the shake in his voice as he controlled his temper, "so the plentiful ammunition in the country won't fit into the rifles you've supplied for us."

Cameron held the clipboard at an angle and made notes and nodded as VD spoke, "I'm very sorry," he said, "I should have checked, but you know, so much to do here," he waved his arms at the plane in front of them, "and I had to get Delvin's handgun too."

Hunt turned and looked sideways at VD.

"What are you writing?" VD asked.

"I am making a note to speak to du Toit, our man on the ground in Varrissa to get you more ammunition. Or make a plan for a resupply. Nothing else I can do now. You boys sure do have a lot of weaponry, enough to have a good Guy Fawkes day."

Cameron grinned at his joke, but his face dropped when neither Hunt nor VD reacted to it.

"I thought du Toit was with the Russians?"

Cameron shrugged.

"What were you saying about Delvin's gun?" Hunt asked.

"Yes, ah, gosh," Cameron looked up searching for the words, he closed his eyes and as if he was remembering an order in a restaurant, "Delvin wanted a Smith & Wesson revolver."

VD shook his head, "Why the hell would he want that in the jungle?" he said to himself. Hunt went and put his hand on Cameron's back and gave him a pat. He felt his anger subside, it was always a quick thing with him, his rage and hate were like a firework, and then it was over.

"Ah, never mind about the rifles Cameron," Hunt looked

at VD as he said, "everyone wants seven-six-two rounds, until they have to carry them," and Hunt winked at VD and the Dutchman nodded and understood the sentiment.

There was a saying in South Africa: *'n boer maak a plan,'* and on foolhardy missions, like the one they were about to embark on, it became more of a mindset. It meant, no matter the obstacle, we'll make a plan. If you wanted to be a farmer in Africa, you better learn to make a plan when things go wrong. It was the only way to survive.

"*Ja*," VD said in agreement, "stiff upper lip and all hey Cameron?"

"Yes, yes, indeed. Jolly good," he said and smiled along with them.

VD and Hunt laughed.

"Tell me more about these plastic crates you're loading," Hunt said to Cameron as they walked towards the cargo plane.

"They're a type of reinforced polymer actually," he said, "they are very strong, but very lightweight, and should be fire resistant, tamper proof and are very, very strong."

"Sounds like they do everything but swim," VD said as he tailed them.

"Oh, they should float too," Cameron said with no hint of irony.

THE THREE OF them walked up to the rest of the group assembled at the bottom of the steps. Maddy was in tortoise shell dark glasses and held her hand up against the sun as they walked over. Delvin, Fabrice and Trevor stood in amongst their personal gear and carry-on items. Each of them had a black backpack full of essential gear. Poncho, sleeping bag, first-aid kits, emergency rations and other survival gear. Hunt had insisted.

They greeted one another and Fabrice gave them a big smile. He was a giant of a man. Hunt was tall, but Fabrice was a head taller. His hand wrapped around Hunt's gently and he felt that it was smooth and soft and his nails were manicured. Delvin's handshake was soft in an altogether different way. With Fabrice you could feel the strength in the palm and fingers, that he was being intentionally gentle. Delvin's hand was clammy and soft like he was trying to squeeze, but couldn't. Hunt stood next to Delvin as VD spoke to Maddy. Cameron briefed Trevor up on the plans and preparations. Fabrice checked his backpack for something.

"I hear you requisitioned a handgun for the trip," Hunt said softly to Delvin without looking at him.

Delvin glanced at the side of Hunt's face and his spectacles glinted in the sun and he swept his long brown hair to the side of the parting.

He cleared his throat, "Yes, is that a problem?"

Hunt shook his head once, "Not a problem, I am just wondering what you're planning to do with it?"

Delvin shrugged, "what do you need guns for?"

"Guns?" Hunt repeated then switched fire, "you said you were Special Forces, didn't you?"

Delvin turned square to Hunt shielding his eyes from the sun and nodded.

"Yes, I did."

Hunt nodded and waited for him to continue, but he was finished and bent down to tie his leather boot.

"So you can help set up camp in the jungle then?"

"I can try," he said as he stood, "I am here to help."

"Roger. Just make you keep that elephant gun in good order and made safe. Last thing we need is some pygmy finding it on the floor of the forest and chasing us down with it, alright?"

"You're the boss, Stirling," Delvin said and smiled. Hunt saw his teeth for the first time. They were yellow nubs, like they'd been worn away and his gums protruded out bulging above the stumps of his teeth. Delvin's face changed and Hunt realised he'd pulled a face at the sight of his mouth. Delvin mock saluted and turned to get away from the awkwardness.

Trevor stood at the front of the group and looked like he was about to say something. He checked his watch and put his hands on his hips.

"Right," he spoke over the machinery on the runway, "I just want to say hell-of-a-job getting everything ready in time. We are still twenty-four hours behind the German consortium, but the Russians and Chinese have had a few problems of their own and are stuck on the ground in Congo, they've formalised an accord to co-operate in their efforts to prove minerals and win the concession. We are in last place right now, but the team ahead of us have stumbled. Don't let them get away! I am counting on you! Good luck!"

The team were all smiling and Cameron put his clipboard under his arm and clapped. Fabrice put his dinner plate sized hands together and went up to shake Cameron's and say well done. Hunt noticed Maddy smiling and looking at him out the corner of her eye. Trevor sidled up and stood beside Hunt, applauding.

"Just bring them back alive, Stirling," he said and patted him on the shoulder twice. "You need to speak to du Toit on the ground in Puerto-Nuevo, get him to go with you on the expedition at all costs, okay?"

Hunt nodded.

"Don't lose him to the Russians or the Chinese."

"Okay," Hunt said and Trevor walked away as Maddy came up to him.

She stuck out a thin white hand. Her nails were short. Hunt took it lightly.

"Looks like we will be up to our eyeballs in South Africans on this trip, Mister Hunt."

"Yes, wonderful people aren't they?" he said.

"Never met a nice one," Maddy said wryly with a grin.

"Lucky for you I am Rhodesian then, isn't it?"

And she held onto his hand for longer than she should have.

"You like to play that card when it suits you, I notice. Some days you're as British as fish and chips, others you act like you've just come off a safari. Which is it?"

She left the question hanging and walked away.

CHAPTER SEVEN

The upper deck of the converted freighter aircraft had eight Business Class-style seats arranged in pairs. Two seats were behind the exit door on the port side and VD made sure to snag the window. The others piled in where they could. Hunt dropped down in the seat next to VD. Maddy was in the starboard corner of Hunt's right shoulder.

She put headphones on and set up her laptop. Delvin and Fabrice also had a row to themselves. After take-off VD ordered a Scotch from the lone air hostess and pulled his bush hat down over his eyes and said, "I am going to dream of finding reefs and reefs of gold. It's the only goddamn reason to be on this blasted mission," and leaned his head against the window and went to sleep. Delvin looked like he was listening to music in the front row.

Hunt and Fabrice glanced at one another, the only ones not listening to music.

"What have you got there?" Hunt asked Fabrice after he caught his eye.

Fabrice held up a thick stack of printed papers.

"It's my book," he said.

His interest piqued, Hunt stood and leaned over to see. It

read, 'Tribes and Territory: Coevolution of Phonology and the Lexicon in Twelve Languages of West Africa.' Hunt raised his eyebrows and nodded, "I have no idea what it means," he said, "but I'm impressed."

Fabrice smiled broadly.

"Do you mind if I sit?" Hunt asked.

"Not at all, please, here."

Fabrice moved some things from next to him and Hunt sat down. Even though it was Business Class, both men's knees were wedged in against the seats in front. Hunt thought it was comical to see two giant men crammed next to one another.

"It is my PhD thesis," Fabrice told him, "I am working on turning it into a book. I want to raise the profile of the study of linguistics in Africa."

Hunt felt the glare on him as Maddy looked through the gap in the seats.

They spoke for some time. Fabrice was from Cameroon in west Africa. His first language was French and he'd moved to Britain when he was fourteen after the Headmaster in their rural village noticed his 'special gift' for physics and languages. Now, he spoke nineteen languages, most of them fluently. And he'd already published several dictionaries and one volume on the history of pre-colonial Africa, "it's kind of a pet project for Maddy and me," he said, and Hunt turned over his shoulder to look at the pretty face behind him and she looked down and away.

"My father wanted me to become a priest," Fabrice said, "and my grandfather wanted me to become a *sorcier*," he looked up at Hunt, "a witchdoctor," he said, translating.

"I have some experience with a witchdoctor," Hunt said and this seemed to particularly impress Fabrice. It turned out that as a child Fabrice had apprenticed with the local witch-doctor in their village, under the close supervision of his grandfather. He said that the particular kind of hypnosis they employed on him still played a role in his life. In his dreams he felt he could tap into the cosmic history of the tribe and immediately recall the unwritten legends and folklore.

"One of the reasons we were forced to move was, that particular witch was convicted of a series of ritual murders in the years before I knew him."

There was a moment of silence after Fabrice spoke those words. Hunt looked over at VD as he slept and remembered back to the visions he saw in the smoke and rasping gargle of the *Nyanga* in the Eastern Highlands. He shook his head and snapped back from the thoughts of the dream. Fabrice watched him intently, but didn't ask. They had been flying for several hours and it was dark outside. The cabin lights dimmed.

"Better try and get some kip," Hunt said.

"Yes, I am tired too," Fabrice said.

"You're so squashed in here Fabrice, why don't you sit next to VD and stretch your legs? He might use your shoulder as a pillow tonight, but you'll be more comfortable."

Fabrice agreed and they swapped seats. He smiled and nodded his thanks and Hunt smiled back. VD didn't shift. Hunt looked out the starboard window at the purple horizon and thought about the mission. He heard Trevor's final words over and over as if they were being spoken to him for the first time, 'keep them safe, bring them back.'

It weighed on him that he was searching for Digger and Langdon. The image of having to assassinate McArthur Gentry in front of Maddy flashed in his mind's eye and he glanced over his shoulder. She was still on her laptop, sat under the beam from the reading light. He put his head against the cool plastic window and closed his eyes.

He thought back to when he first met Digger and how much he owed him as a friend and as a mentor. The first time they'd met was on Hunt's first exercise after he passed selection into the Special Boat Service. They were sent to train in the jungles of Brunei, a tiny nation on the island of Borneo and surrounded by Malaysia. Hunt had felt self-conscious and wary in the jungle, wearing his shining squeaky-new gear, and still had the advice of the Regimental Sergeant Major chiming in his ears, 'it's harder to keep than it is to get. And don't you forget that.'

Hunt had shouldered his Bergen and followed a group of strangers into the dusk dimness of Southeast Asian rainforest. At the top of the trees, it was sunny and light, but hardly any sunlight reached the rotten leaves and mud at ground level.

Hunt had been led to a commune of pole-beds. The radio continuously hissed and food bubbled and plopped in cooking pots. The smell of cigarettes and mosquito repellent hung in the air and dampness clung to everything. It was impossible to stay dry. He'd felt like he'd walked into something from the Vietnam war. Digger had been there, and looked after him from the moment he arrived and kept looking after him until the moment Digger had retired and left the Regiment.

As standard operating procedure in the British Army, they'd been taught to 'stand to' before first and last light. This meant getting up before dawn, squaring away the gear and being ready and alert to fight, before the sun came up. It was prime time for an enemy attack and everyone knew to be ready.

First light in the jungle was at six, everyone should be ready to go, watching their arcs thirty minutes before. Nobody moves in the jungle at night. You can't see anything and ambushes and traps are set.

Hunt had got up. The jungle was silent around him. He put his damp, cold, 'wet kit' back on and it chafed. He waited, 'stood to', until after first light. Birds were singing and the smell of food wafted his way and Digger came up behind him with a brew.

"We don't stand-to out here, Hunt," Digger had said and handed him the tea, "No point really. Not your fault, someone should have told you. Don't worry, I know what it's like to be the new guy."

It didn't stop him feeling like a cretin.

HUNT FELT a tap on his shoulder. The whine and rush of the jet engines and coldness of the cabin pulled him from sleep to awake. He looked out the corner of his eye and saw Maddy. She stood in the yellow glow of the reading light while the rest of the crew slept. She lifted her finger to her mouth to tell him to be quiet and then summoned him to sit next to her.

"Look here," she said, as he sat down and rubbed his eyes, "I think I've found it."

"You couldn't sleep?" Hunt asked.

He looked at her and she pulled a face. He could tell she felt tired.

"I don't expect to sleep too much over the next two weeks," she said. "Now, hush. Look here."

She pointed to a satellite image on the screen.

"What is it?" Hunt asked.

"Listen carefully, okay?"

Hunt nodded.

"Most people think when you look at a satellite image, especially for earth processing you're looking at pictures of the present time, but that isn't strictly correct. At Earth-eye we mostly use remote sensor technology. We look at images of solar radiation and how it reflects off different surfaces. The radiation bounces off the surface and back into space, like a mirror," she said and checked if he was following.

He nodded.

She continued enthusiastically, "Something black absorbs

more radiation. Well, look at this," she said and pointed to the screen.

Hunt shrugged, "I have no idea what I am looking at, or looking for," he said.

"Okay, okay," she said, and lifted her hand to her mouth and thought. "We're looking for minerals, right? Gold, diamonds, platinum, whatever ... Well, untouched rainforest, or *primary jungle*, is what most people think of when they think of a 'rainforest.' Massive hardwood trees with an underlay of palms and ferns and moss holding onto the sodden earth. But, if primary jungle is cleared by man and then later abandoned, a completely different type of second growth takes over. They're softwood, grow fast and they're bamboo-ey and viney."

Hunt grinned. She smiled at him again. She was as animated and excited as he had seen her.

"Well," she said and pointed to dark lines on the image again, "the radiation is different when it has been cleared and regrown, *and* we can tell how old it is!"

"How?" Hunt asked. He was intrigued, but he wasn't sure why yet.

"Because - and this is the interesting part - primary jungle lives for hundreds and hundreds of years, but when it is cleared and left alone it grows and dies every two decades or so."

"So it is layer upon layer of secondary jungle," Hunt said.

"Yes! So, I wanted to check areas where humans might have inhabited the jungle in the past, like the banks of large rivers, the base of mountains and the like. Guess where we find both of those things?"

"Mount Lamia," Hunt said.

"It is a tiny radiation signature we're looking for," she said, "And, looking across something like five hundred thousand square feet of rain forest on the northern edge of Lamia. I can't be a hundred percent sure, but I think I found an ancient city, or settlement, of some kind."

She pointed to the screen and traced her finger along dark grid lines on the image.

"Can you see the dark lines?"

Hunt nodded, "Yes."

"Our software estimates this secondary jungle," she tapped the keyboard and flicked the image over to a graph, "is over six hundred years old."

She looked at Hunt expectantly to see his reaction. Her face glowed, but he wasn't sure what he was looking at.

CHAPTER EIGHT

The aircraft dipped and shook with a shock of turbulence and Maddy gasped and grabbed his forearm. She quickly withdrew it and looked away and blushed.

"Sorry," she said.

"I am not sure I understand."

"Okay, let me try again," she said, "we're looking for mineral wealth, right?"

"Yes."

"If there was mineral wealth somewhere, it would likely be around an established civilisation. Humans have always congregated around sources of wealth. And, we know that gold and diamonds, but especially gold, is brought to the surface near volcanoes."

"Okay ..." Hunt said.

"Urgh," she said in frustration, "One of the reasons Dictator Debby decided to open the race to prove mineral wealth was they found fragments of deposits downstream in the river basin. Which means that there might be minerals further upstream."

"Sure, right, I get that."

"We just don't know if there is any *more*."

"Alright."

"Well, *genius*, if we found evidence of human civilisation, potentially an advanced civilisation for the time period, it might indicate that they were there because of the mineral deposits, and there might be more. A lot more."

"And no-one else knows about this except us?" Hunt asked.

"Exactly! Finally! You get it. We might win this thing!"

Something occurred to her.

"I did mention that Mount Lamia is a dormant volcano, didn't I?"

"No ..."

She blushed. "Sorry," she said between her fingers, "maybe I should have started with that. Mount Lamia is a volcano, and we know that lots of minerals are found around the rifts in the earth that the lava pushed to the surface."

She flicked the image back and pointed to it again and said almost to herself, "If it is a civilisation, it could even be the reason they disappeared. The volcano could have wiped them out."

"Or, they extracted all of the minerals and left after they had," Hunt said.

She nodded, "Yes, that is possible too, but we won't know until we check ..."

"So, you're going to hunt for an ancient lost city?"

"We're going to," she said. "Did Fabrice tell you about his research about the Phoenicians?"

Hunt shook his head.

Maddy went on to explain that the working theory was that Phoenicians, master sailors most likely employed by the Ancient Egyptians, circumnavigated the African continent around six hundred years before Christ was born.

"If they'd managed to do that, it was also possible that they'd navigated up some of Africa's largest rivers, two of which were in Varrissa. It was also possible that they established mines and villages and carried the minerals and wealth back to Egypt," she said.

Fabrice was trying to use linguistic records to trace the movement of Phoenicians from west Africa back to Egypt. As tribes moved, they either conquered less advanced peoples and forced them to learn their language, or if they were traders and merchants, the locals learnt the language to help them become profitable. In this way he hoped to be able to chart their movement and potentially identify other sites that they could exploit for minerals.

"You know what this means, don't you?" she asked, "we might have found evidence of an ancient Phoenician civilisation that lived deep in Africa. It's very exciting!"

She looked at Hunt, "You don't seem very excited," she said.

He stared dead ahead and chewed the inside of his cheek, deep in thought.

"Sorry," he said, "No, no, yes. It is very exciting. I was just wondering ... if it was an old town or village, do you think it could still be being used by people? Maybe more modern people, but still utilising the same settlement?" he asked. He looked at her and held his breath.

"I guess so," she said, unsure. "But, we would probably be able to tell from satellite imagery, because there should be signs of life, cleared forest, agriculture, possibly even smoke from fires."

She flicked the screen to an image of green tree tops and peered closely at the display as she zoomed in, "but, it doesn't look like anything like that. We won't know for sure until we get there, if it even is a settlement, but there is no sign of one right now."

"Stirling," she said. He was deep in thought again and looked at her. "Let's not tell anyone about this little theory just yet, I don't want them to get too excited. You and I can know, and I just had to tell *someone* about it, but let's keep it to ourselves, okay?"

Just then Hunt's eyes darted up, he saw the silhouette of a head looking back at them over the top of the seats in front. Delvin ducked his head back down quickly.

"Sure, no problem," Hunt said to Maddy. He found himself gazing at her engagement ring. She noticed and covered it and moved it out of sight.

"You should think about taking it off," Hunt said gently.

She looked at him suspiciously.

"We don't know what is waiting on the ground for us," he said, "or what is lying in wait in the darkness over the next few weeks. You don't want them to be able to hold it against you, you know? You can't give them any reason to think they can get to you."

She dropped her gaze from his eyes and looked down at the diamond on the ring and it glimmered in the reading light. She winced and pulled it off and put it away.

IT WAS after they landed that the problems started. Hunt stepped out of the aircraft door and felt the heaviness of the air. The warm ocean air gusted and in the still moments it was like being wrapped in a blanket. His shirt grabbed onto his skin and the humid air made breathing difficult. He looked at the others as they stood on the tarmac in heat haze and they were all sweating.

A port authority pick-up truck pulled alongside and the beret-wearing inspector climbed out. He walked straight up to Fabrice and spoke rapidly and in a local dialect. Fabrice held his luggage and carry-on under each arm and looked around at the rest of the party and seemed confused.

"English, please," Fabrice said in more of a demand than a

request. The inspector took a step back and then smiled and showed a gap between his front teeth.

"Big man, eh?" he said good naturedly to VD. "You must open for inspection," he said, more sternly this time.

"I thought you spoke twelve languages," Hunt said under his breath and Fabrice glared at him as Hunt stepped forward and put a hand up in front of the port authority man to draw his attention away from his large African colleague. Hunt looked to the top of the steps, where the air hostess stood. "Fetch the captain please," he said and she disappeared inside.

"Here," Hunt motioned to the captain, "he will show you what you need to see, we are transferring to another plane, but we need to get out of this heat and go through customs, alright my man?"

The inspector eyed him up, but let himself be guided by Hunt to the base of the steps and boarded the aircraft to speak to the pilot.

The expedition team walked into the terminal building and joined the back of the queue for passport control. As they entered they saw about seven soldiers lounging around. They waved flies away from their faces. It was even hotter inside the building.

There was one customs official dressed in a dark uniform and sat behind a wooden lectern checking passports. Behind him, hanging from the ceiling, was a portrait of the dictator of the Republic of Equatorial Varrissa, President Debby Mabosongo in full military dress. His sunken eyes glared out and made it uncomfortable to look at. He was a man who claimed to be a sorcerer, ate the testicles of his enemies, and collected human skulls.

"Purpose of your visit?" Hunt could hear the border control man ask as people stepped up.

There was a small, wiry civilian in a double breasted suit standing behind the customs man. No-one had so far been stopped. Maddy moved past Hunt to the front of the queue and put her hand luggage down. She was holding the paperwork for the expedition and everyone's passports in her hand. She smiled at the customs man and blew her hair out of her face as she stepped forward to speak to him.

"We're part of the -" she started to say.

The customs man put his hand up to stop her and beckoned with his hand for the documents. She handed them over. He set the letter aside and flicked through the passports.

"Purpose of your visit?"

"If you'll just look at the letter —"

"Purpose of your visit?" he said again straight-faced with disinterested eyes. He had drops of sweat on his face that hovered in place and only slipped down his forehead and cheeks when he spoke. It seemed like he was balancing them on his face.

Hunt stepped forward, "Business. We're an official mineral exploration expedition."

The civilian in the oversized suit stepped forward. A small, thin man with a round head. The customs official watched Hunt as he handed the passports over his shoulder to the civilian and tilted his head as the suited civilian whispered in his ear. Maddy looked up and Hunt and he shrugged.

"T.I.A.," he said, "This is Africa."

"This way please," the suited civilian said and stepped back and waved his arm in a wide arc. He was inviting Maddy to go into a customs room behind the lectern. She picked up her bag and went to the door and looked back at Hunt, unsure.

"Go in please," the civilian said as he stood behind her.

"Hold on," Hunt raised his voice, "we're going in together."

The civilian bowed his head and stepped back and

ushered the rest of the expedition into separate rooms. Hunt went in behind Maddy.

A soldier stood behind a steel table. He had a thick Afro, puffed up under a beret that looked new. His uniform was clean and pressed and he stood up straight.

"Bags on the table," he said. He was clear and direct and stared blankly at Hunt. And Hunt stared back at him. This was Hunt and Maddy's first experience with the totalitarian attitude in Varrissa. He'd experienced it before in other African states. It was menacing control from unchecked state power. The same power that had seen whole tribes wiped out in genocide.

A fly flew next to the soldier's ear and he waved it away.

"It's just my personal stuff —" Maddy said, and tried to unzip her bag.

"Ah," the soldier said, "step back please."

She took a step to the side and behind Hunt and he could feel her breath on his arm, she panted in fright.

The soldier unzipped each bag in turn and then opened them and searched through them one by one. He ran his hands along the insides and looked for hidden compartments and then took items out. First, Maddy's laptop case. He lifted the laptop and shook it next to his head and placed it down. He pulled open her camel leather bag and Hunt saw the hint of a smile on his lips. He pulled out a pair of white women's panties and held them up in each hand examining them. Hunt clenched his jaw and stared blankly at this man's chin, looking through him. Hunt was hot. He was sweaty. He was on a short fuse. He said, *stay frosty, boy, you better stay frosty*, over and over in his head.

The soldier placed the panties on the table and pulled other things out of the bag. Then moved to Hunt's stuff. First he took out a bottle of whiskey, and then two cartons of cigarettes. Then Hunt's personal items, things for the field, all packed neatly into plastic boxes and dry bags. The soldier slid the bottle of whiskey to the edge of the table. He put one carton of cigarettes back into Hunt's bag and opened the other one. He put a few packets into his pocket and slid the rest next to the whiskey bottle, all the while, he and Hunt looked directly at each other with blank stares.

"Pockets," he said.

Maddy patted her body, "I don't have any pockets."

Hunt emptied his pockets. Multi-tool, wallet, a single key, and a wad of dollars in an elastic band. The soldier's hand went straight for the notes. He looked up with a sheepish grin on his face and it dropped when he saw Hunt's. Hunt's face had hardened and his right hand was clenched tight in a fist so there were patches of white on the skin. The soldier dropped the wad of money and reached around the back of his waist. He brought it to the front holding a handgun. Hunt itched to take it off him and smash his head against the wall.

Be frosty boy, be frosty.

The soldier put the weapon back in his waistband and picked up the notes. He unwrapped the elastic and counted off five hundred dollars and stuck it in his pocket. He counted off another five hundred and put them next to the whiskey bottle. He dropped the rest on the table. He looked into Maddy's eyes and held her stare and slowly lifted her panties up and slid them into his pocket. He gave a single nod and the tension lifted.

Hunt and Maddy packed their things.

Hunt could feel the rivulets of sweat as they ran down his back. When he and Maddy were finally allowed to leave the confined interrogation room they saw the rest of the expedition waiting for them.

"Did they take the bribes?" Hunt asked VD.

"These boys? Nah, too upstanding for that sort of nonsense. Yours disappear too?"

"Faster than a virgin's dress on prom night."

CHAPTER NINE

Hunt watched as the wiry African in the oversized double-breasted suit gave him a smile and soft wave. The customs soldier handed the sly looking civilian a handful of dollar bills. Hunt just shook his head and put his sunglasses on.

They walked out of the terminal building back into the sun. The aircraft was still on the tarmac with its hinged nose open. As they walked up they noticed the pilot and some customs officials standing in a huddle around something on the ground.

One of the customs lackeys used the butt of his rifle to try and break open the plastic container full of gear. He brought the butt down on the sealed latches like he was swinging an axe. Just before Hunt could react a shout came from the side.

"Hey, you bloody fools, what the hell do you think you're doing?"

The expedition stopped and watched as a tall, gaunt man in jeans and a checked shirt loped up to the pilot and a group of customs people. Hunt saw him walk up to the overweight customs officer they'd spoken to earlier. The lean man put his arms around the customs official's shoulder and led him to the side and away from the group. The tall white man was hunched over, talking and waving his hands. It looked like he was making a strong case, pointing this way and that. The customs official listened intently and nodded solemnly on occasion.

Maddy sidled up to Hunt as he watched, "That's du Toit," she said.

du Toit had combed over brown hair with some signs of grey. He was clean shaven and looked more like an accountant than a mercenary.

"I know this man," VD said, "that's Colonel du Toit from my old 32-Battalion."

"Right. That's him," Maddy said.

Hunt saw du Toit put money into the customs official's hand and they shook on the deal. The overweight customs man shouted and the other customs guys packed up and climbed in the pick-up truck.

"So long fellas," du Toit waved as they drove off and the expedition walked up to where he stood. Du Toit turned to face them with a wide smile on his face and said, gruff and dour, "Howzit?"

du Toit stretched out his hand and shook Hunt's first and then went around the others introducing himself, "Hello, Servaas du Toit, call me du Toit, or Colonel, or just 'Oi'," he said and laughed at his own joke.

When he got to VD he said, "*Ag*, I don't believe it. Johan? How long has it been?" They embraced like old friends and spoke to each other rapidly in Afrikaans.

"Sorry to interrupt," Maddy said and broke up the reunion between du Toit and VD.

"You don't look very sorry," du Toit said with a wink.

"Yes, well, anyway ... could you please explain to me why you paid that man when the jet and its contents are bonded?"

du Toit lifted his chin to VD and walked over to Maddy, he spoke more quietly and led her away from the group.

"*Ja*, about that," he said, "No need to thank me, but I will need to be reimbursed for saving your gear from grubby fingers."

"Where were you ten minutes ago when grubby fingers put their hands all over my lingerie?"

du Toit laughed and said, "Who brings lingerie to the jungle in Africa?"

She had no response, but the heat was making her mad.

"Are you coming with us or not?" she asked and shielded her eyes to better see his face.

"Can't unfortunately my dear, I have a contract with the Russians already."

"I hear they've been held up," she said.

"They'll be here soon enough."

"So what are you doing helping us?"

"Trevor asked for a favour, get your meat-heads more ammo and help get you loaded onto a new plane you're flying into Cote d'Ambre."

du Toit noticed Hunt and said, "Who is this?"

"Stirling Hunt," Maddy said and introduced them.

"You South African?" du Toit asked.

"When it suits him," she said and rolled her eyes and wandered away from the 'boy chat'.

"I think she likes you, eh?" du Toit said with a wink and patted Hunt on the shoulder.

"Rhodesian," Hunt said and felt like he should have added a 'sir' at the end.

"*Ag*, good man," du Toit put his hand out again and Hunt took it, "a word to the wise," du Toit said, and gripped his hand and leaned in close, "the Varrissa interior isn't exactly a picnic spot these days. The Fang tribes in north-west Varrissa are on the war path, they're cannibals you know? Even the Pygmy aren't friendly anymore. They're as likely to kill you as speak to you, if you even see them, that is. Forest people, you won't even know they are there. And the people have been talking about the mountain blowing its top, apparently some witch doctor had a vision and everyone is scared."

"Thanks," Hunt said. It sounded like a piece of cake.

"Anything else?"

"Ah, just the usual, malaria, blackwater fever, corruption. Might be worth delaying the trip a while."

"No can do, unfortunately," Hunt said and released du Toit's grip. He hated long handshakes and his palm was getting sweaty.

"Makes no difference," du Toit said, "the Russians are going in big, thirty-plus people, they're going to clear out the bush and establish a base of operations, explore the jungle as far as they can. Road is almost built already. Probably end up cutting half of it down and selling the timber too."

"Even more reason for us to win this thing," Hunt said, "you should be coming with us."

"You can't afford me Stirling, anyway, you have VD, he's the real deal."

"Yeah, I know..." Hunt said and glanced over at his fat Afrikaner friend as he stuffed tobacco into his pipe and swore when he dropped some down his shirt.

du Toit called over to Maddy, "So? Where is your new aircraft?"

"I thought you organised that for us? Isn't that it over there?" She called back and pointed over to an old turboprop that sat outside a hangar.

du Toit walked over to Maddy and said, "Oh, no! That Fokker is reserved for the Russians."

"What!? No, no, no du Toit. That is *our* plane. Trevor specifically asked you to get it for us!"

"This is Africa my dear, where the highest bidder wins the prize."

She straightened up and her face hardened, "Fine. How much?"

"I can't do that, my dear, it's been secured by the Russians."

"You know goddamn well that is our plane du Toit."

Hunt and VD walked up to the two of them arguing on the runway.

"Come on," VD said, "just tell them we took it from you. They'll never know the difference."

du Toit shook his head and smiled, amused at her frustration.

"How about this," Maddy said and glared at him furiously, "either you give us what is rightfully ours, or after we win this thing, you never work for Earth-eye or any western team again?"

"Come, come," du Toit said, "threats are so unbecoming Maddy, my girl, especially empty ones."

"Urgh! You're so goddamn infuriating. And *don't* call me 'my girl!'" Her face turned red and she clenched her fists. She turned to get away from him. She stopped and turned back.

"How much?" she demanded again.

"A hundred thousand Swiss francs in a private bank account and point-zero-five of a percent of the first year return on primary deposits."

She shook her head, "A hundred grand in Dollars and point-zero-one of the first year's return on *all* deposits fully discounted from point of origin."

"Point of origin," he shook his head, "from the middle of Varrissa? No. Debby doesn't even control Varrissa right now. You could lose it all."

"You're a gambling man du Toit. So gamble. Get in the dirt and weeds with the rest of us."

He shook his head.

"Fine," she said, "straight buyout at two hundred thousand in USD," and stuck out her hand.

"*Ag*," he surrendered, "I'm selling your own goddamn

83

plane back to you anyway," and winked trying to get a rise again.

"And the pilot," she said.

du Toit hesitated, "I have no-one else to fly," he said.

"I'm sure you'll make a plan. Part of the deal."

He shook his head and then her hand. She had her plane. Hunt was impressed.

"You're backing the wrong horse with the Russians," she said to du Toit.

THE FOKKER-50 LOOKED like a model miniature as it stood next to the Boeing 747-400 cargo jet. The customs officers du Toit had bribed lugged heavy plastic boxes onto cargo ramps and transferred the equipment into the smaller turboprop. Maddy supervised the loading and VD helped her. Hunt spoke with the pilot and showed him coordinates from the map of where they were going. He said in a thick Russian accent that, "*Da*," he understood, but Hunt wasn't sure.

"And?" Maddy asked him when he came over.

"He says he understands," Hunt said.

VD showed the customs agents how to tie the boxes down with tie-downs.

"It's going to be too heavy," Hunt said.

"We need it all," Maddy said as she made notations on her clipboard. "Here," she said and handed Hunt the clipboard, "take care of this will you? I need to contact Trevor."

Delvin and Fabrice were next to some gear on the tarmac setting up satellite communications equipment. Maddy went over and sat on the runway and pulled out her laptop to send a status update back to Earth-eye base.

Hunt had a check inside the aircraft. It had a single hinged cargo bay door on its side. VD was inside the hold shifting boxes around and strapping them down with some of the customs boys. He stood up and wiped his arm across his forehead.

"Is this *blerrie* thing going to get off the ground?" he said.

"No idea," Hunt said, "looks like we'll give it a go. We need to get moving though if we want to make the runway before dusk. I don't want to be flying in this thing overnight."

"We about ready to go?" Maddy said as she walked up and looked inside the hold. "My God! Where are we supposed to sit?"

"Wherever you can find a spot," VD said.

The back of the aircraft was filled with boxes and supplies.

"We need to get going if we want to spend the night somewhere safe," Hunt said.

"Right, load up!" Maddy said, "let's go."

They loaded up and Hunt pulled the rear passenger door shut. They were perched all over. The boxes were stacked on either side of the aircraft and strapped down, with a narrow path to the cockpit if you turned sideways and sucked your stomach in. The seats were made from cargo netting attached to rails and made up the metal benches that ran the length of the hold.

The engines fired and the propellers began to spin until there was a deafening rush in the back of the old cargo plane. VD sat opposite Maddy and Fabrice and leaned forward with his elbows resting on his knees. As the plane taxied he shouted over the rush of wind and engine noise, "Colonel du Toit told me about a tribe we can arrange porters from along the river."

Maddy and Fabrice nodded.

"I know some of the customs and local dialects," he said, "but, might need some help with the Bantu languages."

Fabrice gave a thumbs up. VD sat back. He had led expeditions before, for oil companies, loggers and protection for the diamond mines in Sierra Leone. He would do his best to help these people, but as he looked at them he wasn't sure they would survive a week in the jungle without the tons of comforts they had packed into the yellow boxes stacked around them.

The aircraft engines whined and the wings bit into the air and the high pressure under the wings lifted them. The plane wobbled, but they were airborne. The pilot kicked open the cockpit door and signalled to Hunt to put on the headphones at the back.

Hunt grabbed the headset and pulled the mouthpiece down.

"Plane too heavy," the pilot said in Russian accent, "reduced maximum altitude."

"But we are safe to fly?" Hunt shouted into the mouthpiece and everyone looked at him.

"*Da,* safe for now. More fuel. Low flight."

Hunt hung the headset back on the wall and Maddy gave him a quizzical look.

"Never mind," Hunt said with a wink, "we'll make it and you should still have your kitchen sink when we get there."

CHAPTER TEN

Three hours into their five hour journey and the view of the landscape shifted. There was a vast difference between the coast and the interior. They'd been following the Roki River, flying in a north-westerly direction. The river was wide and clean and looked serene from above.

They'd all pressed their faces against the clear plastic to glimpse the might and majesty of Mount Lamia as it glistened in the afternoon sun. It shone like a glass tower in a green desert. The virgin rainforest rolled thick and untouched below them. There was a low cloud that streaked past the windows as they climbed through it. The late afternoon sun threw dark shades over the tree tops and angled through the windows in the back of the plane. Hunt and VD had their weapons out of the carry tubes and cleaned and checked them. Maddy was, as usual, on her laptop. Fabrice read his dissertation. Delvin sat quietly and observed Hunt and VD and looked out of the window. VD kept glancing up and frowning when he saw Delvin watching them.

"I don't like that guy," he said quietly to Hunt.

They were all tired. Hunt yawned and stretched and finished with the weapons. VD packed them away. The noise in the back of the plane was too loud to talk. Then, the plane banked sharply and people and equipment slid to the opposite side. The sound of an explosion detonated outside and the whole aircraft shivered and juddered in the air.

Hunt grabbed the headset and yelled into it, "What the hell is going on?"

Everyone held tightly to the meshing, concern written on their faces.

"Someone shoot us," the pilot yelled back into the headset.

Maddy jumped up and looked out of the starboard windows. Explosions rocked the aircraft and it shook.

"It's flak out there, someone is firing at us!" she yelled as shrapnel hit the fuselage. It sounded like hail on a tin roof.

"Climb, climb!" Hunt shouted into the headset.

"Climbing to twelve thousand," the pilot came back.

The engines whined. The explosions continued around the plane and they hit turbulence in the clouds and Hunt felt the pilot shift heading to the west trying to outrun the guns.

"You need to bring us back on course," Hunt said and pulled a map from his pocket. The plane jolted and shook as he tried to get a fix on where they were. A quick map check and he guessed they were overflying the Moa tributary, where it split from the Roki River.

Then, another huge explosion. The expedition all ended up on the floor. Hunt pulled himself up and looked out. He saw the port engine on fire and black smoke erupting from under the wing.

"We've lost the port side engine!"

He handed the headset to VD and said, "I'm going to the cockpit."

He hurried between the cargo and found the captain fighting with the controls. Hunt grabbed the co-pilot's headset and sat down. The pilot was sending a Mayday.

"We're losing altitude," he yelled to Hunt, "too heavy."

Hunt spoke to VD, "we're too heavy mate, we have to ditch some of this weight. Open the bay door and get the others to help you push it out. I'm coming."

"Is there anywhere to land around here?"

The pilot was fighting the controls and shook his head, "only jungle," he said, "crash in jungle, we die."

"What about ditching in the river?"

"Too heavy," the pilot said.

"We can get rid of some weight. Aim for the Moa," Hunt jabbed a finger into the map to show him where and the pilot glanced at it.

"*Da*, okay. No choice."

Hunt got up and pulled out his multi-tool. He cut the straps that held the cargo down.

"What the hell are you doing?" Maddy shouted over the rush of wind and screaming engine. The smell of smoke was thick. VD cut the straps away too.

"Listen, if you don't ditch this kit we will crash in the jungle and die, so help me!"

She stood, stuck dumb for moment, and then helped Hunt untie the straps.

VD opened the cargo bay door on the side of the aircraft. The wind rushed in and it felt like the pilot had hit the brakes, the plane slowed and the pilot swore and fought to maintain altitude.

"Come on!" Hunt shouted over to Fabrice and Delvin and they started heaving chunky high-tech storage boxes out of the open plane door. Hunt pushed one of the crates out and watched it tumble out like a free fall skydiver to the forest below. The top of the trees were uncomfortably close. Their muscles ached as they heaved the boxes out.

"Prepare to ditch!" the pilot yelled through the cockpit door.

Hunt shut the cargo bay door.

"Get your gear," Hunt said to them, "find the lifejackets

under the seats. We're going to have to swim out so don't carry anything you don't need. Brace before the crash and hold on tight."

He could barely hear himself over the rush of wind and noise.

"What about you?" Maddy shouted and Hunt turned back.

"I'm going to help the pilot."

The plane threw them violently from side to side. Maddy made her way back to the tail and Hunt barrelled into the cockpit and sat down. He could see the river below them and it twisted ominously.

"Tell me what you need," Hunt said.

"Tell me my airspeed," the pilot ordered.

"Uh, one-seven-zero knots," Hunt said.

"That'll have to do," the pilot said and fought the controls, "no landing gear, no flaps. Altitude!?"

Hunt searched the instrument display.

"Altitude!" the pilot screamed.

"Two-fifty! Dropping fast, one-fifty," Hunt said.

"Warn the cabin!"

Hunt turned back and saw the expedition crew huddled in the back. They were holding onto one another and onto the mesh at the back.

"Brace! Brace! Brace!" he shouted. They were about to ditch in the middle of a wide fast-flowing river in a wild and unexplored part of tropical rainforest in the middle of a hostile and undeveloped west African dictatorship. The pilot had to keep the wings level and make sure the descent wasn't too steep. If the nose caught they would tumble and, at that speed, it would be like hitting concrete. The aircraft would disintegrate and Hunt doubted they would ever be found. He turned back and put his arm against the front and saw the brown water rushing up at them.

"Prepare for imp -" the pilot managed as they came in

with speed and the tail caught the water. It acted like running into a wire. The fuselage slapped down onto the water violently and threw everyone forward. The pilot and Hunt whiplashed forward and the pilot smashed his head on the control panel and water sprayed up and over the windscreen.

Hunt felt punch drunk. He felt warm liquid run from his nose and he tasted blood. He looked around the cockpit and saw the pilot slumped forward. Hunt unclipped himself and pulled the pilot's body back gently by the shoulder. His head flopped to the side and he bled from a laceration on his forehead. The plane moved and sloshed in the water and Hunt felt uneasy as he stood. He pulled the pilot from his seat and dragged him from the cockpit.

"Is everyone okay?" Hunt said as he pulled the pilot out, "Get that back door open! Get up guys! Come on, we have to get out before she sinks."

Brown water lapped at the windows. "Let's go, let's go," Hunt urged.

"Grab anything that will float, make sure you have your packs and emergency gear!" VD shouted.

They scrambled to get gear and sort themselves out.

"Once you're out that door, don't stop until you hit the bank. I don't want to scare you, but there could be things in the water, so swim like hell and don't stop."

CHAPTER ELEVEN

"We'll activate the emergency escape slide..." Maddy said.

"Assuming it works," Delvin cut in.

"... And I'll deploy the raft," she said and held up the emergency inflatable survival raft in its orange bag, "We can all climb in and get to shore."

"There won't be space for all of us," Hunt said, "but let's sort that out once we're out. This thing is sinking!"

"Is he alive?" VD asked Hunt and pointed to the pilot.

"I don't know," he said, "let's just get him out."

VD went to the rear door and was about to pop it open.

"Wait, wait, wait," Fabrice said, "before you do, I just need to say, I'm not a very strong swimmer."

VD jammed a life vest into his chest and Fabrice put it on. VD twisted the handle and kicked the door. It didn't budge. He kicked it again. And again. Finally it opened a crack. He gave it one more lunge and it popped open. Brown water sloshed in and covered their ankles. The pressurised canisters fired and the grey emergency slide inflated and folded out on the water.

"Alright come on, climb out, stay on the inflatable."

It was like stepping out onto a bouncy castle. The grey inflatable lay on top of the water with high-tubed sides that prevented the water from getting in and sinking the slide. It wobbled unevenly as the expedition team climbed out. The murky-brown water lapped over the wings and the fuselage bobbed and sank. The team crawled on hands and knees out into the middle of the river on the escape slide. Hunt dragged the pilot out with him and VD followed them.

"I think he is gone," VD said as Hunt grunted and pulled the pilot along under his armpits. The pilot's head was flopped to the side and blood ran down and spread out on his white shirt.

Maddy pulled the ripcord and the survival raft hissed and exploded into an orange and black tube.

"Grab it!" Delvin yelled as it floated away. He half fell into the current and Fabrice grabbed him by the legs and held him steady.

"I need to get in first," Fabrice said and climbed over him, "I can't swim."

Delvin struggled to hold the raft.

"Hold it firm!" VD yelled from behind, "Find something to lash it down with."

Maddy held it and held on and strained to stop it drifting off. Fabrice sat in the back of the raft and looked around in a panic.

"Fabrice! Come and hold my hand and keep her steady," she said. She was so tense and urgent he immediately snapped out of it and did as he was told. He clambered forward and held onto her.

"There are animals in here," Fabrice said and his eyes darted.

"Nonsense, just hold onto me," she said.

Hunt flopped back and breathed heavily from dragging the pilot.

"Help me get him in," he said.

Delvin, VD and Hunt lifted the body and laid it in the raft and his legs dangled over the side.

"There's no space," Fabrice said.

"We'll just have to squeeze," Hunt said, "get those oars out and ready."

The plane's nose was above the surface and the emergency slide was being sucked under. The fuselage was almost gone. The current pulled firmly and steadily like a pack of huskies.

"Get in Maddy," Hunt said and Delvin followed her in.

"Go on," Hunt said to VD, "climb in *ou pal*."

VD waded in and the whole raft swayed and Hunt strained to hold it, his forearms flexed tight and he gritted his teeth.

"What about you?" Maddy asked.

There was no more space.

"I'll swim behind and steer," Hunt said and looked around, "the current is pulling us downstream, you need to row hard and get us to shore at the closest point we can reach."

Fabrice jumped and startled as water splashed on his arm. He looked like he was about to burst into tears.

"Come on let's go! Ready?" Hunt asked and pushed off the floating jetty. The plane was submerged and pulled the slide under. VD and Delvin rowed and Maddy sat close to Hunt and held his shirt sleeves as he kicked hard and spat the silty water out .

"Oh God, oh God," Fabrice said.

"What is it now?" Maddy asked, annoyed.

"Over there," he pointed. They looked over and saw a long, black reptile slide silently into the water.

"What is it?" Hunt asked.

VD looked down at him and said, "Not for nothing *ou boet*, but you'd better kick like hell. We've just seen a crocodile get in for a swim, possibly a meal."

Hunt didn't reply but put his face down and screamed as he exerted himself and kicked hard to get to the bank. Hunt looked back and saw what looked like a black ribbed log floating towards him. He could just see the top of something, like a pair of binoculars half submerged. And then it disappeared below the surface. It was coming for him.

"Get me out of here!" he yelled and VD and Maddy grabbed an arm each and yanked him. He kicked hard and writhed to get in. The whole raft tilted and rocked on the water and Fabrice screamed. As they dragged him out there was a violent thrash and a massive set of jaws breached the water. They pulled Hunt in as the jaws snapped shut. Maddy and Fabrice both screamed and VD yelled at it, "*Fok off jou ...*" and pulled back and away from the water.

The crocodile's lock-tight jaws closed around the raft's tube and the pilot's leg as it dangled. The section of the raft popped with a loud bang and Maddy screamed again, she grabbed the pilot's shirt and held on but the creature thrashed its head and sank back into the brown water. It held onto the leg. The whole raft lurched and Hunt managed to turn around and face it.

"Get off him, get off him, don't get dragged in," he was saying as they moved out of the way. The pilot's limp body slid off the back of the raft and into the water. The raft was sinking. One of the inflatable compartments was burst and water sloshed into the raft. Fabrice was crying. The pilot's body sank beneath the surface and disappeared.

"Paddle goddamn you!" Hunt yelled.

He was soaked. Maddy and Delvin paddled. They aimed the raft at a brown patch of sand on the bank. They glided up to it and Hunt kept a good eye out for more crocs. Everyone stepped ashore. They looked around nervously. Fabrice hugged himself closely and stepped onto the sand and peered into the thick bush around them. Maddy and VD dragged the raft up out of the water.

"We might need this for shelter," VD said.

Just then there was the sound of water spraying from nostrils and a grunting bark. Hunt spun around in a crouch. A slippery-wet naked mole rat looking thing the size of a pick-up truck was coming at them. It chuffed and barked.

A hippopotamus charged out of the water, aimed at Hunt and then switched the direction of attack and went straight for Delvin.

Delvin stood shock still, mouth open, like he couldn't believe what he saw. Hunt ran forward and his feet lost traction in the loose sand and he stumbled. Hunt shouted to Delvin. The beast charged like a slick black locomotive and opened its mouth in a yawning gape of sword-like yellow curved fangs. Delvin turned to move. Hunt grabbed the Smith & Wesson handgun from Delvin's belt and pushed him with a hand in his back. Delvin stumbled forward and out of the animal's way. Hunt's momentum carried him forward and he spun and fell onto his back and brought the handgun up in line with the creature's face. He held it firm in both hands and looked down the sight at the whiskered, flared nostrils of some prehistoric nightmare. It closed on him fast. He pressed the trigger and said a silent prayer that Delvin wasn't just wearing the handgun for show. The .50 calibre round exploded out of the barrel. The hand cannon recoiled viciously and he felt the pain in his wrist. The animal's head knocked to the side, but kept charging.

Hunt fired again. And again. *Ca-boom! Boom!*

The beast stumbled. Hunt rolled to his side. The huge head collapsed and hit the sand where he'd just lain. Chest heaving, Hunt got to his knees. He was soaked wet and breathless.

"Hell!" VD yelled and ran over and grabbed Hunt by the shoulders, "You okay?" he asked, as Hunt stood and dusted himself off.

Everyone glanced continuously at the animal like it was about to get up and charge again. There was a lot of back slapping and nervous laughter and Devlin looked deathly pale, like he'd just come back from the dead.

He was shaken, and had a stupid crooked grin on his face.

"Thank you," he said and Hunt shook his head and gave a single laugh and handed him back the handgun.

"We need you, Delvin," Hunt said, "You're the only one here who can work the equipment to call in a rescue. I'm just a meathead, remember?"

"We must have crashed in her territory," Maddy said.

"Maybe he was just hungry? A hungry, hungry hippo," Hunt said and grinned at Maddy. She slapped him on the chest and couldn't hide her smile.

"First a plane crash, and then crocodiles, and now hippos; what next?" VD said, "I don't really want to stick around to find out."

"T.I.A." Hunt said.

"This is Africa," they all chimed, happy to be alive. The hippo's bloated round body lay in the sand and Hunt saw a cluster of eyes. They appeared on the surface and blinked, dull and reptilian and cold.

"Let's get that raft up the bank and away from this body," Hunt said as crocodiles pulled themselves onto the bank and hissed at one another and attacked the carcass.

Maddy shrieked and the others ran up the beach and into the line of trees. Hunt stood on the sand as the others clambered into the darkness and looked back at the carcass. The hippo's eye was open and fluttered as the crocs pulled at its hide. It seemed to watch him and point out the dishonour of its death. There was the sound of crunching and ripping as the cold blooded animals tore at the flesh.

Hunt looked into the forest. He wanted to get away from the death and sound of the reptiles tearing at the carcass. The forest seemed to beckon them. But also held some hidden death. Some evil lurked in there. An eerie feeling came over him. The dead hippo would guard the expedition's entrance into the forest and into the darkness.

CHAPTER TWELVE

Digger heard the anti-aircraft guns in the distance. The sound was dampened by the thickness of the forest and dulled by the trees, but the noise was unmistakable. The guns rolled like bursts of thunder and without the crack of lightning. Both he and Langdon lifted their chins to hear. Then the soldiers and guards scurried around outside, visible from the wooden cage. One came into the hut and fumbled with the lock to release them. He was in a hurry.

"Government troops," he said curtly, "come."

Digger and Langdon were weak and dirty. The guards weren't concerned about them escaping anymore. They wouldn't get far in the surrounding jungle. The guard stabbed Digger in the back and pushed him forward with the barrel.

"Don't point that thing at me," Digger said with more strength than he felt.

As he turned to admonish the guard he saw a turboprop aircraft fly through a clearing in the treetops. He stopped and looked and Langdon and the guard looked too. The aircraft trailed grey and black smoke from the left engine. And Digger saw a yellow container fall from the side of the plane.

"They're dumping their cargo," Langdon said and put his hand over his eyes.

"They're crashing," Digger said.

"I wonder who *they* are?" Langdon asked.

"Government troops," the guard said forcefully and pushed them with the length of the rifle, "Move. No talk."

Digger saw men hurrying and Gentry issuing orders as they descended into the steep-sided quarry. Gentry stood on top of the stone table where they'd cut Simeone's neck and he waved his arms and pointed in all directions as he gave his orders. Gentry looked to Digger like a bad impersonation of Castro giving a speech. *All dictators were alike in their movements and the way they held themselves*, he thought. Most of them were small and shifty like Gentry too. Digger recognised the tall, stone-faced man standing at the front of the group as they listened to Gentry.

Sergeant Bunting had dark, smooth skin and dressed impeccably. He would fit right in on parade in any western Army. Bunting's eyes darted and locked on his, and Digger glanced away and concentrated on holding his footing as they descended the rough path of loose stones and sand into the pit. After they descended the ledge and walked on the quarry floor Digger saw Gentry hop off the table. The soldiers were in a rabble and organised themselves. Gentry put his arm over Bunting's shoulder and Digger heard him say, "Find the survivors and bring them to me." Gentry let him go and followed Bunting's gaze. He looked directly at the prisoners, at Langdon and himself.

"The Lord Langdon and the Mister Gibson. My guests," Gentry said loudly and moved towards them. Bunting eyed them up and then turned back to his men.

"Spies in my midst," Gentry said as he approached.

Digger felt it was an ominous thing to say and he felt Langdon start to shake involuntarily next to him. Langdon twitched like he was about to run and then decided to stay.

"I can't help it," Langdon said and acknowledged his shivering body.

The two of them stood shoulder to shoulder as Gentry approached. The guard cocked his rifle and stood with it aimed at their backs. Bunting and his section of men, six in total, formed a line and started to chant a marching song. They hummed and heaved and took off at a jog. They moved off at a swift pace and climbed the ledge and into the forest. Digger dared not watch them. He saw them disappear out the corner of his eye. He kept his eyes down and fixed them on the ground in front of Gentry's feet.

"Spies!" Gentry cried. His voice high, and sharp, and harsh.

He held his arm out and pointed at the two prisoners. He glared accusingly. Digger dropped his head further. Gentry spoke while twisting his head to look at the decorated walls of the subsurface stone mine, like he was giving a sermon to a congregation of his followers hidden behind the walls. He stepped right up close to Digger and Langdon and stuck his face close to theirs. Digger could smell his body odour and the creams he put in his hair. A sickly sweet smell.

"Spies," Gentry hissed under their noses, "tell me how you signalled them?"

"That's not us," Langdon started and then stopped when Gentry glared. Gentry stepped back and cast his accusatory finger at them again, and threw his head up like he was summoning God.

"I know it was you!" he bellowed.

The prisoners said nothing.

"Strip them," Gentry said to the guard, "search them. Find the device. Or, if they have nothing, cut it out of them!"

He was paranoid and manic and Digger wasn't sure how much longer they would last with this mad man stuck in the oppressive and consuming darkness of the forest. Lesser men than him would already have lost their minds in the smell of damp mud, smothering heat and strange sounds all around them.

HUNT WALKED up the sand embankment and away from the frenzy of feeding and approached the group. They were together in a huddle and tried to decide what to do.

"It'll be dark soon," VD said, "we need to find a place to make a camp."

They each had their packs of emergency gear and rations, the ones Hunt had insisted they pack, the essentials from a kit list, and they were to be carried with them at all times.

"We've got four rifles and ammunition," Hunt said, "you know how to use one?" he asked and looked at Fabrice and Maddy. They nodded.

They had three golocks. One each for VD and Hunt and they decided Maddy should carry the third. VD pulled out a nylon pouch and ripped the Velcro open. He handed each one of them a morphine auto jet on a string and told them to hang it around their necks.

"You don't go anywhere alone," he said, "even if you need to take a dump," he looked at Maddy.

"What're you looking at me for!?"

"Even if you have to take a dump," he repeated, serious, "take someone with you. You take your weapon, and a golock," he held up the long curved knife, weighted on the end to cut through the forest, "and a compass. Anywhere you need to go. This jungle hates us and it is going to try and kill us," VD said and looked into the gloom that surrounded them.

"We dropped a lot of cargo, over a wide area, out of that plane," Hunt said, "I need someone to come with me and help me find some of it. We can follow the river and try and get some gear."

Hunt looked around. They looked concerned, "Listen," he said and got on his haunches to look them in the eyes, "we get through tonight. We find the rest of our stuff. We send for help and get out of here," Hunt said.

"We aren't leaving," Maddy said.

Everyone looked at her in silence.

"We've come this far, we can't give up now. We're nearly where we want to be, aren't we?" she snatched the map from Hunt and glanced at her global positioning watch and ran her hand along it, "we would have been coming down this river anyway. All we need to do is find our stuff and regroup. It can't be spread that far, what was it? A few miles from when we dumped it to where the plane crashed? And it is all on this bank of the river."

VD looked at Hunt. She's not wrong, his look said to him. Hunt sighed. He knew they needed to stay to find the hostages.

"You're the boss," he said to Maddy, "how about you come and help me find a box of goodies and the others set up camp for the night?"

"I'll come too," Fabrice said.

"Alright," VD said, "Delvin, it's you and me setting up the camp."

"I marked the coordinates of the drops, roughly, but I have positions where we can start our search for the containers," Delvin said.

Hunt nodded to him, "You made a note of our position?" he asked. Delvin gave a nod and showed him the scrap bit of paper he'd written the coordinates on.

"Well done," Hunt said as he looked at the paper, "someone was thinking ... Okay, we all go. Or, we all stay. We can't afford to split up now, and anyway, we can't make camp anywhere near that carcass and crocodiles. They'll attract too much attention. The most important thing to find is our shelter and camping equipment and food, then the comms and survey equipment," Hunt said.

"Let's go. We can follow the bank and set up a camp in a decent place before dark. Anyway, this place gives me the creeps," VD said.

They picked up their packs and Hunt said, "Assume you're being watched all the time," and they trudged off into the darkness. Hunt was at the front, followed by Maddy, both of them swung their golocks at the undergrowth and cleared a path for those behind.

"Cut as little as possible," he said over his shoulder, "we don't want it to look like a herd of elephants stampeded through here."

HUNT MOVED TACTICALLY. He had the butt of the rifle in his shoulder, safety catch off and finger on the trigger on full automatic. They moved for over an hour snaking through the dense jungle to the latest coordinate on Delvin's list. It was slow going. The advantage of a thick canopy was that the growth on the ground was sparse. Hunt knew from experience in Brunei that when the canopy thinned and sunlight reached the ground, the thickness of the vegetation made it so they'd be lucky to cover one mile in five hours.

Hunt tried to move them in the low ground. They came to the crest of a hill and gave the hand signal to stop. The single line column stopped and crouched and VD moved up the line to check on them, like a good Colour Sergeant would.

Hunt dropped his pack and crawled forward to see what lay in the dead ground beyond. He was already soaked from his time in the river and the jungle was sticky and steam drifted off his shirt. He had sweat in his eyes and it stung like a wasp.

Hunt crawled to the top of the ridge and looked out. The

forest dropped away and opened onto a dry plain. It looked like the forest had been cleared by man. He saw tall grasses in clumps around a sand clearing. The forest continued again on the other side. Hunt could see Mount Lamia rising up out of the thick green vegetation off to his right hand side. The summit was ringed in cloud, so he couldn't see the top. The forest was still and the sun still bright against the river and the sand. Hunt checked his watch. It was five o'clock, there would still be enough light for at least two more hours. He inched backwards to rejoin the others and continue on, just as he moved he thought he heard a sound, and stopped and listened.

He held his breath. There were bird calls and the occasional hoarse cough from monkeys in the trees. Then he heard it again. Voices. He looked up slowly and over the ridge. He strained his eyes against the dense thickness of the green on the other side. He saw a metallic glint in the sunlight and something moved just inside the tree line on the other side.

CHAPTER THIRTEEN

Hunt lay very still and pressed his face into the wet leaves and mud. He heard voices again. Men jabbered and talked and the sound carried over the open ground in front of him. Then he saw them step out of the gloom. They walked casually forward and held AK-47 rifles by their sides or over their shoulders and across the back of their necks. Their skin glistened with sweat in the sunlight. Hunt counted four men. They walked forward and scanned the ground. He kept watching.

One of the men, to his right, was hidden by tall reeds from the river bank and called out to the others. The others stopped walking in a straight line and moved over behind the reeds. Hunt was about to crawl backwards and warn the others, until he saw another glint of light. It was just a fraction of a movement. Behind the tree line, in the gloom of the forest, he could make out a dark shape.

It looked like a tall man was standing in the darkness with his arms folded across his chest. He wasn't like the others. He didn't move immediately towards the excited shouts coming from behind the reeds. He peered across the stretch of no-man's land. Hunt wondered for a second if he was looking at him too. He held his breath again and dared not to even blink.

"What's taking so long," Hunt heard someone complain from behind him and swore silently in his head. *Shut up, just shut up*, he thought, *you're going to get us all killed*. The figure across from him crouched on his haunches. Another man that Hunt hadn't seen made his way in front of the tree line to the crouched shadow. The man in the shadows stood and Hunt saw that he was tall. They moved off to the reeds and Hunt's view was blocked again.

He reversed himself inch by inch until he was clear of the line of sight from the open ground. He turned and cut swiftly back through the undergrowth. VD saw him first and Hunt lifted his finger to his mouth. Maddy opened her mouth to speak and VD put his hand on her shoulder and stopped her. They all closed in on Hunt in a crouch and he whispered urgently to them.

"Be very still, be very quiet," Hunt said, "there is a group of soldiers investigating our gear and they are not, I repeat, are not friendlies."

Who they were, he had no idea, but he wasn't going to wait around to find out. The team looked at him and waited for their instructions.

"VD will stay here with me," Hunt said and nodded to VD, "the rest of you need to get as far away from here as you can. He pulled out a map and checked their position. He knew that in thick rainforest there was likely to be an error in the range of around ten to thirty feet. He marked the position and got Delvin to confirm where he thought their position was. And Hunt marked the rendezvous points on each map, spaced a mile or so apart.

"Take your compass, and head north-east. Cover your tracks. Stop at the first rendezvous and wait for thirty minutes. If we haven't found you by then, go for the next one and wait an hour. If we still haven't found you do it again and stay there until we find you. Whatever you do, get deeper into the jungle."

He saw that Maddy wanted to argue, but she thought better of it.

"We'll make sure they don't follow and we'll try to slow them down if they do, then we'll come and find you, but only when we are sure there is no-one on our tail. Any questions?"

They shook their heads.

"It's about surviving the night," Hunt said.

HUNT MADE his way back to the top of the ridge. VD stayed where he was. The others moved, crouched over and quiet, deeper into the thick darkness of the unknown. Hunt crawled forward. He scooped soil and mud into his hands and rubbed it on his face. If he had camouflage cream he would have applied it thickly. All he wanted was to remove the shine from his skin. Skin is a reflective surface. The only purpose of the thick paste of cam cream was to remove that shine. Hunt rubbed the mud on thick. Shape and silhouette could also give him away, but slow movements minimised the risk. He inched forward until he could see and held his breath.

He saw the tall, dark skinned man as he talked to another more junior, ragtag looking soldier. Four men walked past behind him and struggled under the weight of one of the yellow cargo boxes. They carried it off into the forest opposite Hunt's position. The taller man talked and signalled with his arm toward the river. The soldier turned to look and nodded.

"He's going to walk the bank and search for the crash," Hunt whispered to himself. That meant they would be back. Hunt wondered, did they have vehicles? If not their base of operations couldn't be far away, and that was dangerous. If they did, they were better equipped and more professional than he hoped they would be.

The tall man checked his watch and the young soldier nodded. The soldier was barefoot and in a baggy military shirt. Just then the taller man glanced in Hunt's direction and stared. The young soldier turned his head to see and shielded his eyes from the sun. The tall man didn't move and just watched. Hunt held his breath again. He dared not breathe. A bird cried out and flew out of the trees and over the clearing to his front. Both men looked up at it. It distracted them enough that they looked away and they turned back to finish their conversation. After the tall man turned to leave, Hunt scooched backwards, and down the ridge.

He went back to VD and briefed him about the situation. They would wait for the young soldier to pass by, make sure he was following the bank, and stalk him from behind. They needed to know where he was going and how he would react if he found the crash site. They prepared themselves and fanned out. They made their way in a slow and controlled manner and moved tactically toward the river. They kept their space between one another and found a position under cover and with visibility to the bank. As Hunt lay and waited, and the insects attacked his neck and legs, he hoped he was right. He had a nagging doubt about what he had seen. Was the tall one really signalling for his junior to search the river bank? He tried to avoid checking his watch. Then he heard it. Something moved to his left.

The junior soldier he'd seen wandered into sight. He was ambling, not paying attention. He climbed over fallen trees and swung between the branches. He looked to be in his own world. *Not a care*, Hunt thought. Hunt knew VD was off to his right without being able to see him and they both waited. The young soldier was in shorts and carried his AK-47 rifle over his shoulder. The weapon looked clean and operable, which was a surprise. To Hunt, this meant that this group, whoever they were, whatever their allegiances were, had discipline and training. It meant they knew what they were doing and someone was sound enough to check on the men and make sure they did the right things. They had leadership.

After the soldier had passed him and they'd given him time to move off, Hunt got up and slinked over to VD's position. They didn't need to speak. VD must have heard him approach and got to his knees and then stood up. Hunt signalled with his hand the direction of travel and that he would follow. VD simply nodded and moved off silently through the undergrowth.

They kept seeing glimpses of their quarry as it moved through the trees to their front. He wasn't paying attention and didn't seem frightened about being alone in the forest. Hunt wondered if this meant he expected the others to be back? He didn't want to be surprised by soldiers coming up behind them and glanced over his shoulder. VD stopped in front of him and made the signal at waist height to stop. Hunt pulled up next to him. He could see the soldier's head through the trees. He'd stopped and was looking at something.

VD signalled that that was the crash site. They decided to move around to get a better view. They boxed around the position out of sight and moved around to the area where they had entered the forest before. Hunt could see the soldier clearly. He had a curious look on his face. To his front was the carcass of a hippopotamus. Around the carcass, four crocodiles lay with bloated bellies, and pink-headed vultures circling overhead. The smell of death clung to the air. The reptiles carried the stench of blood, and the smell of the carcass turned in the heat. It was already starting to rot. Flies landed on the croc's heads and flew around the open wounds of the hippo. The soldier looked back down the path he had come down.

"What's he going to do?" Hunt wondered out loud and

VD shrugged.

He could make out the end of the escape slide in the middle of the river. It was mostly submerged. The soldier wasn't acting like he'd seen it yet. He moved around the animals and kept a wary eye on the crocodiles. They were full and lazy and one of them slinked into the water and disappeared. As he rounded the carcass and got a better view he stopped and looked out. The soldier looked directly at the grey inflatable in the river. He looked back down the path he had walked down, and then turned again. He took a step forward and the crocodile to his front hissed.

He said something under his breath and went to cock his rifle. *He's going to shoot it,* Hunt thought. If he did, and the other soldiers heard it, they would come running. Hunt looked at VD, he'd already lifted his black M-16 rifle and used his index finger to release the safety. Hunt waved his hand at VD and told him not to fire. He got up and moved forward silently. His heart beat faster and his breathing was shallow. He didn't want to get shot in the middle of the African jungle. The soldier heard a twig snap behind him and he turned his head. Hunt charged.

As the soldier turned and pointed his weapon, Hunt slammed his fist into the boy's bottom jaw. His head and neck snapped to the side and he fell in the lump where he'd stood. The crocodile turned and hissed again with its mouth fully open and showing rows of straight teeth inside a cream-coloured mouth.

"Ouch. Damn," Hunt said as he shook his fist loose and massaged his knuckles.

VD came up behind him and picked up the AK-47 and made it safe.

"I'd probably have done less damage if I'd shot him," VD said and indicated the crumpled body lying in the sand.

"Didn't you once tell me to always go out there and knock 'em dead?" Hunt asked.

CHAPTER FOURTEEN

"What are we supposed to do now?" VD asked and gestured towards the body.

"Better check he is alive," Hunt dropped down and touched the soldier's neck. It felt warm.

"It's gonna be dark soon," VD said.

"Let's get out of here. Try and find the others. I think they'll be at the second RV," Hunt said and checked his watch. He took the sling off his rifle and tied it around the soldier's wrists and pulled on the knot to make sure it was secure.

"Why don't we just kill him?" VD asked and nodded to the forest. Hunt took it to mean that they could hide the body and no-one would ever be the wiser. Hunt handed VD his weapon and bent to pick the prisoner up. He heaved him onto his shoulder and slung him like a bag of cement.

"Let's question him first and find out who the hell he's working for, and what they are doing carrying all of our gear away," Hunt replied.

"Ag, alright," VD agreed and they trudged up the sand bank and into the thick gloom and darkness, "always too much sense making from you. I prefer to act first and react later," he said as he passed Hunt and took the lead.

THEY WERE MAKING good time and traipsed through smelly mud. Insects clicked and screeched around them. The smell was in Hunt's nose and he couldn't properly wipe his brow and get the sweat out of his eyes. He felt the limp body stiffen and he knew the soldier was awake.

"Hey, hold up a second," Hunt called to VD whose sweaty back faced him. He had one weapon slung and carried Hunt's rifle. VD turned around.

"This bugger is waking up," Hunt said as he stopped. When he did the soldier thrashed like a landed shark. He writhed and kicked and screamed out in a piercing cry that broke and went high pitched and silent at the top. His legs kicked violently and, as Hunt set him down, sunk his teeth into Hunt's shoulder.

"Ah! Bastard!" Hunt yelled and held onto the crazed prisoner. VD lifted his rifle to warn the soldier and he took off and ran. Hunt tried to grab him, but he slipped through his arms as they closed and he ended up on all fours and watched as the slight black frame scampered into the bush.

"Get him!" VD yelled.

Hunt looked at him for a split second, and shook his head in disbelief at what he was about to do, and took off like a sprinter. He was a big, heavyset man, but once he got his thick muscles pumping and stride length going he could move fast. The prisoner twisted his head as he heard Hunt crash through the undergrowth and screamed as he ran. He ran with a fast waddle from side to side, unable to use his tied up arms, and it slowed him. Hunt chased him down. He'd disappear from view and then reappear as Hunt broke through the ferns and broad-leaved

Alocasia. The soldier ran into a thick branch that overhung the path and it knocked him to the side. He stumbled and fell on his knees and scrambled to get up. As he did, Hunt crashed through the branches behind him. The prisoner bellowed in fright again and got up to run. Hunt dove and tackled him around the legs. He fell forward and kicked out furiously.

"Calm. Down. Now," Hunt said with effort as he tried to keep hold and restrain him.

The prisoner kicked and lashed out and screamed with bare teeth in Hunt's face. His eyes searched frantically around and looked for a way to escape or for a weapon. His body went rigid and his head and neck were stretched all the way back. It happened in a moment. Hunt could see the whites of his eyes as he strained his neck to see. He'd spotted something. Hunt was on top of him and tried to grab his wrists. The soldier pulled away and reached behind his head. There was a rotten log on the floor behind him. It crawled with big red ants and insects.

And then Hunt saw what it was. A beetle the size of a child's fist. Long and black with dots of yellow on each leg and two bright yellow spots on its back. Hunt was the one trying to get away now. He knew, whatever it was, it wasn't safe. The bug's yellow-spotted legs crawled in midair and its needle-like mouth opened and closed as it looked for a victim to punish.

Hunt knew there were venomous insects in the forest and he moved to get away, but the soldier pressed the insect into the bend of his arm. The solider pushed it deep into the soft skin at his elbow pit and immediately he felt the sting and pain. Hunt yelled out and managed to brush the prisoners arm and the bug away. He looked down at the fold of his arm and it was red and raised and welted. The prisoner had a sick smile on his face and Hunt dragged him up and pinned him face down. He untied the guy's arms and retied the knot behind his back. Hunt stood, and felt lightheaded, but pulled the prisoner upright. Hunt forced him to march back through the foliage and thicket.

"What was it?" Hunt asked him through gritted teeth as he steered him through the dense darkness, but the prisoner wouldn't respond. Hunt realised that this prisoner was calm now and he started to worry. Hunt stumbled and then saw VD, and he looked anxious.

"You found him," VD said, and then, "Hell! What happened to you?"

"Why?" Hunt asked.

"You don't look very well," VD said and pulled the prisoner away. He didn't feel well. Hunt pulled him down by the arms and the prisoner sat with a thud. Hunt noticed the boy's eyes were glazed over and he stared at him with a smirk on his face. His confidence unsettled him.

"What did you do to him?" VD asked the boy.

He didn't answer. VD lifted the rifle and aimed it between his eyes.

"Tell me, or I'll blow your brains out the back of your skull. Now. Speak," he commanded.

The soldier looked away and then said, "Your friend going to die. White-eye assassin bug," he said and lifted his chin towards Hunt and then pursed his lips and shook his head, "very dangerous."

Hunt was doubled over in pain. He turned his arm so VD could see the inside of where he'd been bitten.

"The little shit stain stabbed me with an insect. It hurts, VD. Badly."

Hunt looked up and saw the concern on VD's face. He tried to stand. He had a pain in his stomach and a burning at the back of his throat. He felt like he was going to vomit and wiped the sweat away from his brow.

"Come on," Hunt said and gritted his teeth through the pain, "we have to go and find the others."

"Okay," VD said hurriedly.

He gave Hunt the weapon without the sling and said to the soldier, "if you shout, you die. Understand? I didn't even want to bring you ..."

The boy nodded and rose when VD lifted him. They walked and Hunt followed behind. The left side of his body, where the bite was, had collapsed. The muscles felt sore and weak and the bite mark had risen to a red welt. He took shallow, rapid breaths and shuffled along behind them. The rifle felt heavy in his arms. He blinked and his vision went misty.

"Wait, VD," he called out, or thought he did. VD didn't stop. Hunt put his hand on his knee, the other hung loosely, and he looked down at the mud and soil to catch his breath and focus his eyes. He looked up and VD was coming back towards him with the prisoner.

VD looked concerned.

"I need to rest," Hunt said, but he wasn't sure if he was making words. His mouth felt like it was full of fur. VD helped him lean with his back up against a tree, and checked his watch, and looked at the prisoner. Hunt could see the round black face still smirking at him.

"Go find them," Hunt said, "leave me. Come back."

He was breathless. VD shook his head to protest, but seemed to realise that he was right. VD cocked the rifle and set it across Hunt's lap.

"I'll be back. Don't go anywhere," VD said and patted him on the side of the face.

Hunt gave a pained half-smile and said, "I'll be here, sitting pretty."

———

VD DISAPPEARED into the undergrowth and Hunt waited. He glanced at the trees and rubbery plants and leaves around him. His vision faded. It got fuzzy on the outside and closed in on him. He felt like he was in a tunnel. *I want to stand*, he thought and pushed to get up, but collapsed back down. He didn't know if he'd been there for an hour or seven hours. There was almost no light to guess the time. His head flopped to the side and his heartbeat felt faint and distant, like it belonged to someone else.

He jolted. He looked around wide-eyed and frantic. His tongue was puffy and swollen. His vision blurred and darkening, his thoughts lacked sharpness. He felt drunk, and then he realised he was going to die. And just as he'd thought it, a dark shadow moved in front of him. *The reaper*, he thought. He shook his head from side to side to clear the haze and the shadow was gone. Hunt looked up and saw the brown thin body of a man. He blinked hard and thought it was the venom playing with his mind. Then a shadow in a loincloth stepped forward and Hunt went to raise his rifle. It felt like lifting a boulder. The shadow's arm came out and pushed the barrel of the weapon away. Hunt dropped the rifle and his head collapsed to the side again.

CHAPTER FIFTEEN

VD used the prisoner as a ram and pushed his enemy through the thick foliage. The young soldier was uncooperative. VD didn't care about leaving signs and he didn't care if this scrawny rag-wearing rebel lived or died. In fact, he preferred it if he died. VD marched them through the forest on a bearing and barely deviated, until he heard a shout to their front.

"Halt, who goes there?" came the challenge.

VD recognised Delvin's voice. He stopped and took a knee behind the prisoner.

"It's VD with a prisoner," he shouted back, just loud enough for them to hear.

"Oh, thank God! Come on, we're over here," Maddy called.

VD stood and pushed the boy forward and followed the sound of their voices.

"Oh, my goodness," Maddy said, "*who* is this?"

"Here," VD said and pushed the soldier towards Delvin, "take this bastard and get him something to drink, make sure he doesn't escape. Tie him up and watch him carefully, he's shifty."

Delvin took the prisoner and set him down with his back to a tree and poured some water from a bottle into his open mouth. Maddy came up close to VD and stood next to him and looked into his face. She had her hands on her hips and wiped perspiration from her lip and then held her hands up.

Her eyes followed his and searched his face.

"He's sick," VD said quietly, "I had to leave him."

She took him by the upper arm and led him away from the others. Fabrice watched them go.

"What do you mean, *you left him?*"

VD explained what had happened and looked at the top of the trees as he did. He was feeling guilty and unsure of himself. And it was getting late. It would be dark soon.

"How far, where is he?" she questioned.

"About an hour back down the path I've just beaten through the jungle," VD said, "As soon as you've finished chatting, I am heading out to go and find him."

He said it with more aggression that he intended. He was feeling threatened and accused. She stood for a moment and looked at her feet and crossed her arms in front of her chest. She dropped her bottom lip and shook her head.

"No," she said.

"What do you mean, *no?* This isn't a discussion lady, I am going to find my friend. Full stop."

"VD, no you aren't. Christ! Look around. It'll be dark soon. We have no camp. We have a prisoner with us now. You said so yourself, no-one moves around the jungle at night."

"Well, I'm going. You can do what you like," VD said and moved to walk past her.

"And me too," Fabrice said and stepped closer to them.

Maddy took a step back to let him into the circle.

"We don't know who those men are or what they want," she said.

"That's why I brought him," VD said and pointed at the soldier on the ground, "get him to tell you. Make him do it."

He gritted his teeth. The light faded and VD moved to get himself ready. Maddy continued the discussion with Fabrice and chewed the side of her cheek and bit the side of her nail as they spoke. VD watched them out the corner of his eye as he checked his gear, and listened to Delvin as he talked with the prisoner.

"Who are you? What's your name?" Delvin asked and crouched in front of him.

"Micheal," the boy said.

"Like, Jackson," Delvin said and smiled.

"No, like the Archangel, Michael," the boy said and Delvin's face dropped, admonished by this child. Delvin looked down.

"What are you doing here?" Delvin asked more quietly and unsmiling.

"God's work. We are fulfilling God's plan for his people. And we are here to stop the invaders and the Devil, like you," the boy said.

He spat the words. His face and eyes filled with disdain. Delvin got the message and stood up and moved away.

"*If* he tries to run, kill him," VD said to Delvin as he walked past him.

Michael spat at the ground between his feet and closed his eyes and laid his head back against the trunk. VD stood and cocked his rifle.

"Let's go," he said to Fabrice. Maddy chewed her cheek and stood with her hand on her hips and watched them go. The forest was darker now. The small shafts of light in the treetops dissipated and at ground level it was murky. The darkness rolled in like an evening fog over the sea. VD and Fabrice set off through the fog of green leaves and left the camp behind.

Hunt dropped in and out of consciousness. His head flopped against his chest and then he would wake up immediately alert and lift his head and look around. He felt like he was floating through the jungle and then floating like in a dream. The pain in his guts burned. He imagined a wasp as it zipped inside him and stung the lining of his lungs and stomach.

Bloody thing, I need to get it out. And then there were small men all around him. They had him under the armpits and flew him face first through the forest. It was dark all around and thick ferns and large wavy leaves from some rubbery plants rose up and brushed past him like headlights of vehicles on a dark freeway. He felt he was going to be sick.

"Stop, stop," he called out to the shadows that carried him through the forest, but they didn't respond. *Maybe I'm dying,* he thought again and wondered if this was the journey his soul was taking. He hoped he would see his mother and father on the other side. He wretched. He wanted the wasp out from his insides. It felt stuck at the bottom of his throat. It made it hard to breathe and he tried to expel it, but nothing came. He wretched again. He thought he heard voices. A strange language. But, also like something he recognised. Or maybe he used to speak it as a child, before he forgot and learned to speak like everyone else.

They stumbled out of the darkness. They were panting, their hands and faces cut and they were out of breath. They broke through the thick foliage and back to the camp. VD rested with his hand on his knees and gulped the heavy air and wiped his brow. It was difficult now to make Fabrice out in the blackness.

"What happened?" Delvin asked, seemingly more to break the silence than anything. It was already clear.

"We couldn't find him," VD said, "it's too bloody dark and I could barely see my hand in front of my face."

He knew they were looking at him, but he couldn't make them out properly. VD felt the anger rise inside him. He stood up and breathed deeply and looked over to where he knew Michael, the rebel prisoner, sat.

"And it's all that bloody bastard's fault," VD said and pointed and stepped to the middle of the camp.

"It's God's plan," the boy said matter-of-factly.

Maddy came over to him.

"What do we do?" she asked quietly.

"We have to stay here tonight," VD said, "first thing in the morning, I will go and search for his body. He'll be dead by the time we find ..." he choked and couldn't finish the thought. She touched his arm to try and soothe him.

"I'd better get to work," VD said. He collected himself and stepped away to start sorting himself out. VD got to work making an A-frame hammock. He went into the darkness and used his golock to hack violently at branches and lengths of wood. In theory, he needed four lengths of wood, five to six feet long. He'd lash them together until he had two crosses that could support his weight. He stuck two poles down the length of his hammock and put it in-between the X-shaped support poles. He leaned up against a tree directly opposite the tied up prisoner. Michael watched him through slits in his eyes as he rested his head back against the tree.

"I'm watching you," VD said.

"And my God is watching you," the child soldier said.

VD used bungees to secure a shelter sheet over the top of the A-frame. He made sure Michael was covered too. The last piece was the mosquito netting. Sleeping without it would be madness. While he was fixing the last of the bungees, Maddy came over carrying a waterproof bag. The others had set up the tents from their packs.

"You know we have one for you too," she said and put the waterproof bag down under VD's hammock.

"Nah, thanks," he said as he strapped the last of the shelter together, "I need to watch the boy. He's trouble. But, you can give him a camp bed and sleeping bag if you have one."

She looked over at the prisoner. He seemed docile. She picked up the bag and went to crouch opposite him.

"I'm Maddy," she said to him.

He said nothing.

"Do you want a sleeping bag? Are you cold?" she asked.

He didn't respond and VD came up behind her. VD grabbed the sleeping bag and turned away.

"You'll get this if you talk, if not, I'll leave you out there for the gorillas."

"I am not afraid of you," the boy said, "I am not afraid of the darkness. I fear no evil, for the Lord is with me."

"Tell me who you work for," VD said and turned back.

"You already know."

"Listen, I'm not playing with you. Tell me what I want to know and you can eat tonight, if not, I will feed you to the wolves," VD said.

Delvin appeared in the shadows behind them. VD sensed him and glanced over his shoulder and then back at the prisoner.

"And, I know why you are here, white man," the boy said.

VD shook his head, "Fine. Sleep on the ground then. When you are ready to talk you can have this," and threw the sleeping bag under his hammock.

Fabrice heated some emergency ration packets from a portable fast boiling gas canister. He handed them out. Delvin took one over to Michael and fed him from the steaming packet and spoke to him quietly. The prisoner ate and VD shook his head. He was frustrated. He patted his pockets for his pipe and searched for his tobacco.

"Come on," Maddy said to him in a hushed tone, "what're we really going to do with him?"

"We can decide tomorrow," VD said, "first we need to find Stirling, or even just his body; then we need to find out what that rebel knows, why they were where they were and what they want."

Maddy shot a look at Fabrice. He was silent and listened.

"We'll take turns guarding him and the camp tonight," VD said, "in the morning we will make a new plan. We need to find the communications equipment and make a call for help."

CHAPTER SIXTEEN

Hunt was delirious. He fought off the hands that held him down. He was in the gloom of a reed hut. The walls were dried grass wrapped together tight with homespun rope. He yelled out and screamed.

"Hell! I'm in hell!" He looked around wild-eyed.

The dark faces danced and moved in the flames. His vision was blurred and closed in on him, like the darkness in the surrounding forest. The smell was of dried mud and tobacco. A potbellied old man, wrapped in a brown toga, hobbled in and leaned on his walking stick. Another followed behind. She was small with ears that poked out from the side of her head like an elf. She was bald except for a tuft of hair clumped together on her crown that stuck straight up like it was made from twigs. They both stood and looked at Hunt in the flickering flame of the hut's fire.

"Who you dye?" the old man said and prodded Hunt in the side with his walking stick, "Whetin day 'appen?"

The small woman walked up to the side of his straw bed and smiled. Her teeth were ground down into fine points, like needles.

"Dis big boss man," she said, "he wan no, what 'happen?"

Hunt struggled to get up and cried out. Hands held him down from each side.

The twig-haired woman put her hand on his forehead and wiped away the sweat and smelt her palm. She flicked her tongue out like a snake and licked her palm and tasted his sweat.

"Witch rot bilong kaikai," the old man said.

The woman opened Hunt's eyelids between her forefinger and thumb and peered into his pupils. He lay back and sighed.

"Me witch," she said into his ear, "'dis pygmy Chief. You white devil. Come wit evil spirit."

Hunt shook his head.

"No. No. Me no come evil spirit. Me attack," he said and fumbled over the pidgin English words. He thrust his arm up to show her the double bite mark left by the assassin beetle. She grabbed his arm and examined the bite mark closely. Hunt's head flopped back in exhaustion and his legs kicked out in pain. The old witch jabbered in bantu to the girls by the side of his bed. She sent them to get medicine and they left the hut.

———

BACK IN THE CAMP, VD lay on his hammock and listened to the intense night-time noise of the forest. It seemed like a competition to see which animals could make the worst sounds for the longest time. The beetles trying to outdo the crickets. The crickets fighting with the frogs. The birds shouting down the monkeys. The others were zipped in their tents. VD had finally covered the prisoner in a sleeping bag and mosquito net. He couldn't see the boy, but he had his weapon and head torch to hand if required. Fabrice was on watch, then Delvin, then VD. He decided to try and get some sleep while he could and shut his eyes and let the screeching and clicking and crying put him to sleep. It was fitful. He tried to roll in his hammock and it would sway and he would wake. The blackness of the night made it so he couldn't understand where he was. Until he heard the voices talking out in the darkness and remembered and his heartbeat slowed and he calmed and went back into a troubled sleep. As he drifted he heard murmuring. Delvin was on watch and talked to the prisoner.

Delvin's neck strained as he looked over his shoulder at VD's A-frame. Then he heard the light snores and turned back to Michael. It was eerily dark around them. The prisoner sat quiet, wrapped in Hunt's sleeping bag, and he looked out at his captor. Delvin couldn't see his eyes, but he could feel his stare. Full of hate and anguish. Delvin wasn't interested in all that. He had his face buried in the backlit screen. He stared at it and pressed the thick rubber buttons. It bleeped and he pressed his thumb on the side to lower the volume and cursed under his breath.

The prisoner shifted his weight.

"I feel you staring at me like some hooded snake in the dark," Delvin said without looking up.

"You are the only snake here," Michael replied.

Delvin looked up and stared at where the sound came from. His skin glowed whitish-blue in the light from the screen.

"I know you," Michael said, "from the moment I see you. You are a snake. You are the ones who crashed, I know this. You need to escape, rescue from this jungle. Why the woman think you need materials, when the snake have a phone ..."

"This isn't a phone," Delvin started, "it's a ..." he held it up and shook it as he thought of what else it could be. It buzzed in his hand and he looked down at it, then stood and walked hurriedly into the bush.

CHAPTER SEVENTEEN

THE CLUBHOUSE, LONDON

Soames hadn't heard from his operative in days and it made him nervous. When he was nervous, he worked. His nerves, and the slow inactivity of his stately Richmond home made him pace the rooms, rubbing his chin and muttering, and it agitated his Parson Russell Terrier, Reverend. The dog followed him around with his ears pricked in concern.

So, Soames stayed at work where he could pace in peace. He was usually the last one left in the office at this hour. He had his coat draped over one arm and his hat in the other and leaned to flick the light switch. The overhead fluorescent bulbs tripped and it was dark in the passage. He went to leave, but saw yellow light coming from an ajar door and he went to see. It was Sir William's office. He checked the time and went up and tapped on it lightly.

He heard a voice and pushed the door open and moved in. Sir William was finishing up a phone call. He hung up the receiver as Soames went into the office. Sir William had his head in his hands and rubbed his palms against his forehead.

"Goddamn it," Sir William said.

"I was just leaving and saw the light on, is everything alright?" Soames asked.

"Goddamn it," he said again into his hands.

Sir William dropped his hands and gave a loud sigh. And, only then, noticed Soames' presence.

"Gerry, what the hell are you doing here? Ah, never mind. Christ! It's all gone to shit."

Soames stood in the office and held his coat and hat and wondered if he should leave.

"You don't look very well, Sir William, when was the last time you've slept?"

He didn't respond. He was staring at his desk. His hair was ruffled and his collar open. He might not have washed, Soames thought.

"It's coming apart at the seams," Sir Williams said. "The bloody Prime Minister knows - *somehow* - it leaked. Before long, the press, the nation, Christ!"

Soames opened his mouth.

"She wants blood. She wants their blood. She is furious. It could be the end of me, Gerry ..." Sir William said and looked up at him.

He looked in a sorry state. Almost sad.

"Sorry about your man," Sir William said.

Soames moved into the office and walked up to the desk, eager like Reverend, ready for a walk.

"Have you heard something?"

Sir William looked down and away, "Doesn't matter."

"Sir William, have you heard something? Something about the Boatman?"

Sir William looked away and shook his head, "They're all dead Gerry. Forget about it. It's over."

"But how do you know? Did someone tell you?"

Sir William's eyes seemed to clear and he sat upright.

"Think about it man, for God's sake! They're lost in the jungle with a cannibal. The Prime Minister has the Chief's testicles in a vice and she isn't letting go. It is over!"

"Yes, sir," Soames said and pressed his finger into the desk to emphasise his point, "But, *how* do you know? Where has the intelligence come from? How do you know they are lost in the jungle?"

Sir William glared at Soames. Soames lifted his finger from the desk and straightened up. He held the stare. Sir William seemed to bare his teeth, like some dogs when you touch their food.

"You think I would send your blunt instrument in, to run amok, without a contingency? Is that what you think? Is that the thinking that gets me into this chair?"

Soames paused. He let the personal jibe go, but put it away for later use.

"Don't tell me you aren't in touch with the man on your own mission? Gerry, Christ! Don't tell me that ..."

"So you have intelligence *from* the ground that the mission has failed and the expedition is dead?"

Sir William stared.

"Yes," he said, defiant.

CHAPTER EIGHTEEN

REPUBLIC OF EQUATORIAL VARRISSA, WEST AFRICA

He hadn't strayed far, but for thirty minutes, Delvin thought he was lost. He stumbled around in the dark using the satellite phone as a torch. He tripped over something and fell onto his hands and swore under his breath. He was panicked and knew he couldn't yell out. He fumbled in the dark and as he got to his feet he thought he heard a cough. He froze. He stayed still, half-upright and waited and listened. He heard it again and stood up, he angled his shoulders towards the sound and headed right for it. He dared not change course and pushed through ferns and brush, he stumbled again and swore and almost before he knew it trundled into the middle of their camp.

He was still for a moment. He heard VD's snores and he was relieved and elated. Finally he was safe and could relax. He smiled to himself. And then he heard the snigger from behind him. It was a high pitched chuckle and it tore his pride to the bone. He turned and went closer, up to the covered mound of sleeping bag, leaning against the tree. Delvin jabbed his index finger into it and under Michael's chin.

"Who do you think you're laughing at?"

Without missing a step Michael said, "At you, the snake in the dark who gets himself lost in the trees," and gave his high-pitched laugh again.

"Shut up," Delvin commanded through gritted teeth. He was tired, muddy and felt disgusted.

"No, I will tell everyone what you did," the prisoner said. He was defiant. It took Delvin aback, he dropped his hand away from under the chin.

"You wouldn't."

"I will, right now. I will wake them and tell them that you have a phone and you made a call."

"Or, what?"

"Untie me and let me go."

Delvin looked around at the tents and at the A-frame and thought about it. Sleep noises rustled out from each of them.

"Who did you call?" The concealed voice came out of the sleeping bag. Delvin snapped out of it and turned back.

"What the hell do you want to know that for?"

"So you did make a call ... God sees all."

"You are not God, little rat."

"You are a snake, crawling on your belly, tricking the others."

Delvin was furious. He dropped the satellite phone and clenched his fists. He felt the Devil rise inside himself.

Delvin heard the intake of breath and the prisoner started to shout "Wake ..." but he never finished. He swung a closed fist and felt it knock into skin. And another. And another. Through gritted teeth air hissed out of his mouth. Michael's limp body fell to the side and slumped and Delvin was on top of it pounding it with his fists. The punches started high above his head and fell straight down, like sea birds dropping in for fish. The impacts felt like he was kneading dough. Each shot was heavier and landed onto something softer than before.

Out of breath, chest heaving, Delvin stopped. He looked around quickly, he was frightened and snapped out of the rage. He didn't know what to do. He put his hands under the sleeping bad and felt Michael's skin. It felt warm. He was still alive.

But, not speaking so much now, are you?

Delvin went through the steps in his head. Either way the truth would come out. *Unless ...*

He pulled the sleeping bag away from the boy's head. He looked at the shape in the dark. It moaned. He was coming around. Delvin clenched his jaw and slid his finger's around the soft, doughy neck. He strained and closed his fingers and gritted his teeth. He tightened his grip until he felt the tough, fibrous airway collapse. Michael's eyes opened in fright. His brain's final wakening against the dying of the light. Hands tied behind his back, he struggled and gasped, but no air passed under the constricting python-like fingers and the body went limp.

CHAPTER NINETEEN

Hunt had spent most of the night convulsing on the dried-reed bed. His vision was blurred. He was blind, but for the shapes and shadows that moved in front of his eyes, and he feared he would always be like that. He felt like he was looking through a net curtain at shadow puppets. The flames were warm on his skin and the fever made him uncomfortable. He wanted to swim in a cold lake. The girls held him down when he thrashed and tried to go outside, and then he would become very cold and the fire provided no warmth. He was afraid he would die of cold or exposure.

The witch was there with him. She hummed softly to herself and instructed the women. She chewed, always chewed, and spat the concoction from her mouth onto a metal plate and held it over the flames. When the spasms seized him, his whole body went rigid and hard as stone. His muscles tensed to their maximum. He thought they would tear apart as he exerted, like a sprinter crossing the finish line. His stomach squeezed without him wanting it to. He felt tension and pain. He couldn't breathe during the convulsions. The veins popped out of his neck and his eyes bulged and his face went red. As his body jackknifed in pain he thought it would never end. Finally the venom released its grip on his nervous system and he was able to gasp a deep lung full of smokey-thick jungle air. And it was the sweetest thing he'd ever tasted. The hushed tones of the girls let him know it was serious and they were scared too. And all the while the witch sat brewing her broth and chewing the bark and roots.

VD THOUGHT HE HEARD SOMETHING. He opened his eyes and the forest around him was damp and dark. He heard a commotion under the beetles and crickets and other creepy-crawlies.

"Hey!" he yelled out in the confused sleepy tone of someone awake after only a few hours sleep, "What the hell is going on?"

He fumbled for his head-torch. Found it and pressed the rubber button. The white beam lit the scene and it took him a moment to adjust. He saw Delvin coming towards him. Delvin shielded his eyes from the light and VD thought he saw blood on his hands. Delvin saw him look and wiped his knuckles on the back of his trousers.

"Listen, VD," he whispered as he came up to the A-frame, "the prisoner, the kid, he tried to escape and I stopped him, I had to stop him, but ..."

"But what?"

"... I think I killed him."

VD was quiet and narrowed his eyes.

"I didn't mean to, honest, it was a mistake. I hit him and he fell and I think he hit his head on something hard, or something."

"... or something," VD repeated, "right."

"Well listen, you said yourself, you thought he was better off dead, right?" Delvin said. And VD felt like he was trying to bargain. VD rolled himself to get up and Delvin put up a hand, "No, don't get up, I've got this. I'll cover the body. The others don't need to know."

VD pushed the hand away and smelt his palm. The metallic smell of blood. That sticks in your nose. Zinc and iron.

"Move away," VD instructed. He got up and Delvin stepped back. He checked his watch. It was early in the morning and the sun should be in a few hours.

"There is no need, really," Delvin said.

"Stop talking," VD said gruffly. He didn't have time for this snivelling little shit's excuses. "Show me the body," he instructed.

"Over there," Delvin said and pointed and looked at his feet.

VD grabbed his rifle and cocked it and pushed his way past Delvin who shuffled backwards and disguised a wry smile. VD twisted back quickly to see if he had noticed correctly and Delvin's face dropped.

"I see you," VD said, matter-of-fact, with the white head-torch light shining on Delvin's face. VD left the others in their tent and walked to the far edge of the camp. The sleeping bag was lying crumpled near to where Michael had slept. VD followed the trail of stamped foliage and walked fifteen feet into the jungle where the body lay.

"His hands are tied," VD said.

Delvin hadn't moved from where VD left him near the A-frame, and he looked up when VD spoke.

"Come here you shyster," VD said a little above a growl. Delvin wandered over. "You think I want to talk to you from across the campsite? People are sleeping," VD said and turned back to the body.

"His hands are tied," he said again and pointed at the body. Michael was on his left side. His body looked long and stretched out, his head hidden away by large leaves and bush.

"Yes," Delvin said.

"Well ..."

"Well, what?"

"Well, how was he supposed to escape with his hands secured behind his back?"

Delvin shrugged and shook his head.

"Where are his footprints?"

"What?"

"His footprints," VD said, "where are they?"

"I dunno."

"You said he was trying to escape?"

"Yes."

"Well, how did he get to where he is, if he didn't run, like you say? There would be tracks."

Delvin shrugged again.

"I see," VD said.

VD walked back to the A-frame.

"Where are you going?" Delvin called after him, "What are you going to say to the others?"

THE GIRLS HELD Hunt down while the witch poured the glossy mix of saliva and chewed up root into a metal cup. She used her fingers as a strainer and left the mangled clumps of now soft root shavings on the plate. His eyes were blurred and he startled when she put her small, rough hand on his forehead and forced his head back.

"White *karamapim tok*. You mus' drink dis," she rasped.

She lifted the mixture to his lips and poured it. It was like slurping a cold oyster. The salty slime made him gag, but she forced it down him like he was an ill child.

He started coughing.

"Yes, dis working," she said and picked up the metal plate.

Hunt rolled onto his side and coughed violently. He felt

like his body wanted to vomit, or that whatever she had given made his body want to vomit it up.

"Here," she said to him in between bursts of ragged dry coughs, "You must' dis chew. No swallow down, only chew," she said and gnashed her teeth to make the point. She held the metal plate of crumpled root and bark out to him. He shook his head. The witch gave the girls a look and they put their hands on him and held his head back. Hunt clenched his teeth shut, but the witch forced the dried bits of root into his mouth. When it was in his mouth, the hands let go, and he rolled onto his back and groaned and chewed the rough textured shavings.

The effects of the drug didn't take long to manifest. Hunt was still physically blind, but vivid images appeared like a hologram in front of him. The witch ushered the girls outside the hut and sat down next to the fire and brewed tea. Hunt's eyes were open and darted across the images. They were showing him something. They slid into view like a projector screen. Moments from his past. Moments he'd forgotten or were suppressed somewhere. These images were different to memories. He was there, but instead of these things from his past happening to him, they were images of cracks in his experience that *just* happened. The deep and profound realisation set in, that all of the experiences of his life, that made up his identity, shaped him, he'd taken to heart and felt afflicted by, were things that had happened to him, and he had taken personally. Whereas what he was seeing on the screen in front of him was seeing that these things just happened. They didn't happen *to* him. There is only a personal attribution if you choose that. Images of childhood, his parents arguing, pets dying, friends crying and graves being dug. The cracks closed as the images swished by only to be replaced by more and more experiences of hurt, pain and anguish. The images started to move at pace, flicking like on a screen, and swooshed like a rollercoaster going down a tunnel straight into the earth, he was going deeper and deeper into his psyche the closer he came to the present. The last one froze on his colleague, his comrade and his friend Johan van Driebek, like a train arriving at a station. The image flashed up and he felt a surge and all of the toxin and poisons came out violently. He rolled on his side and threw up all over the floor.

VD SAT CUTTING a point onto a stick with his knife. It was dawn and Maddy and Fabrice stirred. The shallow light filtered down and changed the complexion of the camp. It looked like there had been a struggle and Delvin moved around to make things more usual. He picked up the sleeping bag and went to cover the dead prisoner's body.

"Don't touch him," VD said. It was loud and forceful and Delvin threw the sleeping bag so it covered the corpse. Maddy stepped from her tent and stretched her back.

She looked at VD's face and asked, "what's going on?"

Delvin made himself busy and watched out the corner of his eye and VD stood up. The other tent unzipped and Fabrice stepped out and muttered his good mornings. Maddy looked between VD and Delvin.

"Well, is someone going to tell me?"

VD walked past Maddy towards where Delvin was making himself busy and said, "Tell her." Delvin straightened up and adjusted his glasses. They stood and waited and the silence dragged.

"I ... I ..." he paused and changed tack, "he tried to run, he was going to give our position away, I had to," Delvin said.

"Oh, Delvin! What have you done? Where is Michael?" Maddy put her hand over her mouth.

VD walked out of the camp a ways and pulled the red sleeping bag and dropped it back in the camp. Maddy and

Fabrice hurried to look and when she saw the body she gasped and put her face into Fabrice's shoulder. He held her and looked at the body. He couldn't remove his eyes.

"That's what we're dealing with," VD said.

"But he tried to escape!" Delvin argued.

"With his hands tied behind his back, in the dark," VD said.

The quiet hung in the air like the smell of mud and death.

"God, I feel dirty," Maddy said and wiped her hands on herself like she was washing.

"Listen, sorry," Delvin said, "I ... I was alone. What else was I supposed to do?"

"How about not kill him?" Fabrice said, "Wake us up?" He shook his head. "I find this horrendous."

"We needed him," VD said, "don't you get that? We needed what he knew. Now, if those soldiers find us, we killed a prisoner. How do you think they will treat us? What about any prisoners they might have? How will they treat them?"

Delvin's eyes locked straight on VD like a shot, and a wry smile rose on the corners of his lips.

To VD, there was something strange in his reaction.

"Are you actually smiling?" Maddy asked. Disgusted, she walked away and went into her tent.

Delvin's face dropped again and he looked at the ground.

"Do they have other prisoners, VD?" Delvin asked.

VD didn't answer.

"What do we do now?" Fabrice asked.

CHAPTER TWENTY

VD bent down and picked up the sleeping bag, he went over to Delvin who turned away.

"What? You can't even look at it," VD said and pushed it into Delvin's arms.

"Okay, he's had enough," Fabrice said, and looked pained for his friend and colleague,

"Enough?" VD repeated, "No. He hasn't even started. Instead of staying here and heading out to find *my* dying friend, we have to pack up this camp. While we do that, Delvin here is going to dig a grave for that dead prisoner," he lifted his chin towards the feet sticking out of the bush.

"Bury him? Why?" Delvin protested.

"You're going to argue with me?" VD said.

"He's right," Fabrice said, "We need to get rid of the, um, evidence, if those soldiers find us," Fabrice said.

VD nodded. "Thank you."

"I don't have any tools," Delvin said.

"I don't want to hear it," VD cut him off, stern and uncompromising, "make a plan. Use your goddamn hands for all I care."

Delvin's face flushed red. His lips were pursed tight-shut. He stared up at VD from under his brows.

"Don't look at me like that," VD said, "I'll knock your bloody block off. Get to it."

Delvin turned away and went to the body. VD went to his A-frame to pack. Fabrice did the same.

———

HUNT SAT UP. He finally felt good enough to move. There was no wasp stinging his gut anymore. He felt a warm and happy affection for the twig-haired pygmy witch. She sat over her cauldron at the fire and brewed him herbal teas.

"What's this one, fruits of the forest?" he asked as she handed him another steaming metal cup.

"You naughty *buksop*," she said and tutted at him.

He felt full of energy. His muscles were tired. He still couldn't keep any food down. But he buzzed. His mind glowed like a hot poker. His body ached, but he felt better than he had in weeks. The witch yanked at his wounded arm and dressed the bite. She stuffed a paste into the bites she'd ground together in a mortar and pestle.

"Ouch. Ah," Hunt cried, only half mocking, as she covered the wound. The remedy hurt more than the venom.

She looked up at him and went, "Shh," and slapped his wrist and he grinned.

"You big *pasin* man, how you can say 'ouch'," she chided.

The chief and his entourage came into the hut. The witch stood and bowed slightly and Hunt bowed his head. There was a younger man with the chief. He had wide, symmetrical features. His mouth was a straight line under wide interested eyes. The chief spoke to the witch and they conversed in their language.

"Chief, he say, hunter-man see some people in forest. White *karamapim tok*. White devil, like you," the witch said.

The young hunter spoke up, he looked at Hunt and raised an arm off to his side to show the direction. He spoke to the witch and she translated.

"He say one big gorilla with *karamapim tok*."

"Those are my friends," Hunt said. They had to be. "Can you take me to them?"

The witch didn't translate, instead she went and pushed him back down by the shoulders.

"No, no, you sick *pasin'* boy. You stay. You rest. We find big gorilla later."

Hunt winced and blew the stench from her sharp toothed mouth away from his nose, and laughed at her midwife-like care.

"Me show you the *karamapim tok*," the young hunter said and patted his chest, "Me, Batwa." and looked at the chief. He nodded solemnly.

"Bah!" the witch said and turned away. She wiped her eye and Hunt realised she was crying.

"There, there," he said and comforted her, "no need to cry." She turned and hugged him around the waist.

"Let's go, Batwa," Hunt said.

"You naughty *pasin'* boy," she said between the tears. She let go of him and Hunt shook hands with the chief and with the young hunter. They ushered him out of the hut and he ducked under the low entrance and groaned in pain. His body hurt and he felt the stabbing sensation in his muscles where the venom left its mark. He stepped through and stood tall and was greeted by the whole village. A line of pygmies in loincloths, tufts of bushy-curled hair and big-bellied snotty nosed children waited for him. He greeted them warmly and they smiled shyly and turned away. The chief followed him out and they grew quiet and serious. Their village was hidden amongst the trees and flora and concealed by a curtain of thick vines and bamboo cultivated with the help of the jungle of centuries. The shyness of the pygmy had kept them alive and Hunt shook each of their hands in turn and said thank you for saving his life. After the chief said a few words and the witch blessed him and the hunting party. They set off in the direction the young hunter set.

VD GRUMBLED as he pulled his A-frame apart. He stuffed the tarp and sleeping bag into his Bergen and swore to himself. He was aware of Maddy watching him, as she packed her own tent away.

"Sorry," he said out loud to let her know it was a lapse. He was frustrated by what had happened and anxious about what happened to Hunt. He was thinking about how they would get his body out of the jungle and who might attend his funeral if they did.

"VD, could you give me a hand?" Maddy asked and he looked over to see her struggling to re-pack her gear. He dropped what he was doing and wandered over. He inspected the situation and got on his haunches.

"Thanks," she said, "always struggle with these bloody things," and made a face.

Something caught VD's eye and he stood up.

"Hey, where is Delvin?" he asked.

Maddy and Fabrice shook their heads and looked around.

"I'm sure he is around here somewhere ..."

"*Ja*, but he is supposed to be getting rid of that body. Who knows what animals will come sniffing around. And if those bastard rebels find us with that thing still lying there ..."

He moved to the body to see where the missing expedition member was. VD pushed apart some leaves to see if he could see beyond them. All he saw were the sunken black eyes of the child soldier and the white-purple skin that sagged off his cheeks. Ants and flies buzzed around and the jungle had started the process of decomposing the flesh.

"Urgh, *fok*," he said and held his nose against the putrid-sweet smell. Where was this bloody bastard? VD walked around the corpse's feet and studied the earth. He saw some broken shrubbery off to the left and stepped across.

"VD, where are you going?" Maddy asked, but he was too focused on looking for a ground sign to notice. He saw footprints. He stepped around and looked up at the wall of jungle in front of him. Had Delvin run off? Or if he hadn't, what was he doing? VD looked back at the camp and saw Maddy watching him. He wondered if he should get his gun. No need, Delvin didn't have the minerals. He went to look for him.

———

THE WITCH'S potion gave Hunt a buzz and he was alert and tuned into the environment, but his body lagged his mind. He sweated and held his side for the cramp as he kept pace behind the pygmy hunter. The hunter moved like humans in jungles were meant to move. Silent, fast and he left no trace. Hunt, meanwhile, thrashed along, snapped twigs and brushed past bush and trees. He only had one thing on his mind: to get to VD. The pygmy would just turn back and give him a curious smile from his straight mouth and then jabber to himself.

"How far now?" Hunt asked.

"No far now," the pygmy said and beckoned over his shoulder without looking back.

The guy must've been late for a date or something the way he was moving.

———

VD PUSHED some large heart-shaped palm leaves apart and thought he heard something. He stopped and listened and held his breath. There was a murmur from up ahead. He checked the ground sign again and saw mud pushed up to the side of a footprint. Someone slipped a bit there. Probably stumbling around in the darkness; go figure. VD's heart rate picked up and he breathed through his mouth. He moved in slow precise movements and felt like he was stalking a deer. The murmur ceased, and then started again. VD moved some leaves and stepped past. He crouched low and inched forward. He was behind cover and peered into the green. A man paced just beyond. VD watched. He saw Delvin's swept aside brown hair and oversized spectacles. VD couldn't hear what he was saying. Who the hell was he talking to?

CHAPTER TWENTY-ONE

VD moved closer for a better view. He kept his eyes on Delvin and shuffled on his haunches. He parted the leaves with his hands. Then, *snap*!

A twig cracked underfoot and Delvin spun around suspiciously and aware. He froze. He was holding something to his ear and looking in VD's direction.

"Hold on," VD heard him say.

Delvin reached around his back and pulled out the chrome Smith & Wesson hand cannon he'd requisitioned for the trip. He had his hand to his ear and swung the handgun from side to side and scanned the bush around him.

VD couldn't move, couldn't breathe. Then, Delvin struck. He dropped whatever was in his left hand and hurtled through the foliage. VD was taken off guard. He saw the crazed eyes and the chrome weapon coming down on him like a hammer. Delvin swung the piece of metal like he meant to take VD's head off. VD unbalanced and fell backward onto the muddy ground. His hands went up against his ears and his forearms took the impacts of the sharp edges of the gun. Delvin screeched and flailed wildly and his chest heaved. He realised he wasn't doing the damage he wanted. In the space, VD fought to get up, but heavy around the midriff and with a man on top it was difficult to get purchase. His hands slipped in the rotting leaves and Delvin struck again. Delvin dropped the handgun and spun himself onto VD's back, like a dancer around a pole. He got behind VD and locked his forearm onto his windpipe and around the Dutchman's thick neck. His other arm came under VD's left armpit and clamped against Delvin's wrist. VD was in a choke hold and felt his windpipe crush under the pressure of Delvin's blade like forearm. VD's hands came up and tried to pull, but as he did, Delvin locked his legs around VD's waist and compressed his gut. Like a mouse in a python's squeeze, VD felt his energy levels drop and with every movement the snake tightened its grip.

———

HUNT STOPPED in the pygmy's tracks and they both listened.

"Did you hear that?" Hunt whispered.

The pygmy put his hand up and leaned towards where the sound came from.

It was a screech, but not animal, human.

"Come on," Hunt said and moved past the pygmy. He went from a fast walk, into a jog and then started to run. His left side dragged in a limp still damaged from the venom. He heard the young hunter behind him as he barrelled through the undergrowth. Something drove him, he didn't know what, but that was an unnatural sound.

A cry that would make a mother's face drain white.

———

A SOUND CAME out of VD that he hadn't heard himself make before. A gag-like wretch and his mind recoiled in the horror that it was not getting any oxygen. He fumbled behind him trying to get a purchase on Delvin. VD felt the hot, sweat stained body behind him as he strained against the heft of the rough Afrikaner. He felt himself slip. Stay awake, stay awake.

"Now you can die you fat ..." Delvin said. VD dug his nails into Delvin's forearm. He grunted, acknowledging the pain, but the grip remained. VD scratched and tore at him, until his strength gave out. VD's eyes lost their vision, like a train entering a tunnel. The last thing he saw was Stirling Hunt smashing through the undergrowth towards him. His last thought ... They lied. Life wasn't flashing before his eyes and now he had to see this oaf, rushing at me, as the last thing he'd see before he died.

Hunt moved hard and fast through the forest towards the noise. He didn't see the bodies on the floor in front of him. He charged straight through and tripped over the tangle of flesh and stumbled forward and fell into the mud and rotten foliage. It knocked the wind out of him. Hunt scrambled to his hands and knees and looked up and saw the spectacle wearing communications man choking VD from behind. His first thought was to ask what the hell was going on, that quickly left and he moved towards Delvin. Hunt's face hardened and his jaw locked. Delvin released his choking grip and VD's body slumped. He back-pedalled to get away and get up before Hunt got to him.

Hunt rose up like a grizzly and Delvin's heels slipped in the soft ground and spun like tyres in the mud. Delvin looked around frantically and spotted the chrome handgun in the leaves. Hunt saw Delvin's eyes fix on it and he lunged. Delvin was faster and moved like a striking snake. Delvin's hand snatched out and grabbed the heavy, metal handgun and went to raise it up. Hunt saw the wry smile on his lips and realised he was helpless. Delvin was going to put the huge calibre round through his chest, like Hunt had, through the head of the hippopotamus. He'd saved this man's life. He'd trusted him. And now he was going to die on the forest floor next to his friend and comrade at the hands of this traitor. Delvin's finger tensed against the stiff trigger. Hunt's face scrunched prepared for the impact. He knew what gunshots felt like.

There was a shout, "Hey!" and Delvin hesitated. Maddy and Fabrice burst through the bush and into the small clearing. Fabrice went up and snatched the handgun away from Delvin. He had surprise and shock on this face and put his face in his hands and started to sob.

"I'm sorry, I'm sorry," he said, over and over.

"What the hell is going on?" Maddy asked, desperate and at a loss.

Hunt scrambled forward and put his ear to VD's chest and listened. He couldn't be sure. He tilted the Afrikaner's neck back and blocked his nose and blew air into his lungs twice in quick succession. He put one hand on top of the other and compressed his chest and counted as he did, "one, two, three, four …" and then blew into his lungs again. Hunt felt the knot in his throat and his eyes watered. He also felt the rage rising inside him. He glanced at Delvin who sat rocking back and forth with Maddy patting him on the back and rubbing his shoulders to comfort him. Fabrice came and kneeled and got a fright when he saw the young pygmy hunter step out from the trees.

The pygmy hunched down next to Hunt while he tried to revive VD. The pygmy held what looked like soil and clumps of rotten earth. The young hunter clapped his hands together and Hunt smelled a strong and overwhelming stench. The bitter and sickening smell of ammonia.

The pygmy held his hand under VD's nose and waved them over his face and the big Dutchman coughed and took a big inhale in. He opened his eyes in fright and rolled around fighting the men off and tried.

"It's okay, it's okay," Hunt reassured him and VD looked into his eyes like he was seeing him for the first time.

"Where am I?" VD asked. Then his mind clicked, his face relaxed and he sank back and breathed. Hunt stood up.

Maddy was still comforting Delvin.

"He tried to kill VD," Hunt said.

Maddy stood and looked down at a person she trusted as a member of her team. Delvin's eyes rose to meet hers, and his expression changed.

He knew he was caught.

Hunt heard something off to the side. It sounded like static or a faint voice. He started to look for the source. He scanned the ground. Delvin jumped to his feet and rushed over to him and tried to pick something out of the mud. Hunt pinned him against a branch and said through gritted teeth, "I am warning you, try it again, it'll be the last thing you ever do."

Fabrice came over and put an arm on Delvin, and nodded to Hunt. Hunt bent down and picked up the black satellite phone. It was wrapped in a protective, clear plastic case.

All eyes turned to Delvin. They stared at him full of accusation and disbelief.

"You lied to us," Maddy said, "you had a line to the outside world this whole time."

Delvin looked away.

"Who is on the other end?" Hunt asked and lifted the phone to his ear.

"Come in, over," he said and tried to sound like Delvin.

"Who is this? What's going on zero-alpha? " the voice on the other end came through faintly and with static behind it.

"Roger. Zero-alpha. Confirm mission, over," Hunt said and scrunched up his face. He sounded unconvincing. There was silence and the line was dead.

Hunt punched the keys and held the phone to his ear. He heard the deep drone of the connection trying to connect. Someone picked up. The voice was garbled and electronic, like a dial-up modem.

"Soames," Hunt heard through the noise.

"Gerry, it's Stirling," Hunt said, almost a shout.

The relief and of getting through and the sense of closeness to the outside world was overpowering. The line whined and beeped and Hunt heard they could hear the odd word, but the poor audio made it impossible. He looked at the screen and it showed one bar of connection. Not enough. Hunt felt his fury build.

"You're a double agent," he said and turned to face Delvin and used the satellite phone as a pointer. "Who're you working for?"

Hunt walked to where Delvin stood, his back to the branch. Fabrice turned slightly and Delvin pounced. Delvin broke free of Fabrice's hand and snatched the Smith & Wesson from Fabrice's belt.

Delvin waved the gun and shouted, "Stand over there! Get back! I'll use it."

Hunt put his hands up and the others did the same. Delvin turned to VD and said, "get up, go stand with the others."

He looked more rat-like and disturbed than usual.

"What's the plan, Delvin? We're in the middle of a jungle," Hunt said.

"Shut up!" He waved the gun again, "Get moving, back to the camp. Where's that pygmy gone?"

Hunt looked around, but couldn't see the young hunter. He must have sunk back into the forest and made himself invisible.

"Who was on the other end of the line?" Hunt asked.

Delvin sneered and shook his head, "You really don't know? But you should know that shouldn't you Stirling?"

Maddy looked at Hunt and furrowed her brow. She was confused. Hunt wondered if he meant MI6?

"You're all expendable," Delvin said and added a sarcastic, "Sorry."

"Expendable?" Fabrice repeated.

"Surplus to requirements," Delvin mocked, "Orders are orders. It's time to join your precious Archangel in heaven, so *now*, I need you to go back to the camp in a single line. Move it!" Delvin shouted all high pitched and screechy.

Fabrice flinched and started to move. Hunt put his hand on his chest to stop him.

"We aren't going anywhere," Hunt said.

Delvin raised the handgun and fired. The .50 calibre exploded. *Ca-boom!* Birds took flight and there was a high pitched whine in Hunt's ears.

"Let's go!" Delvin screamed at them.

And then Hunt saw a group of African men come out of the bush and trees behind Delvin.

"Let's not," a tall, good looking man in fatigues said. His voice was firm and deep. And Hunt recognised him. The same man that had been standing in the shadows of the clearing on the day they crashed. Delvin spun around.

"Put the gun down," the tall, dark skinned man said.

Delvin looked like he wanted to say something, he changed his mind and raised the pistol. The African didn't move. Delvin aimed and went to yank the trigger. His eyes were wild. Hunt had seen that look before. Men on operations who felt there was no hope. It was all over. Nothing to care for. Going all in at the poker table with no cards.

The African flicked his index finger down, like he was signalling the start of a race, and a volley of AK-47 rounds slammed into Delvin's torso. They hit him like a combination of punches. His chest split wide open. The sounds of the gunshots clanged out around them. The tall African stayed where he was and watched as Delvin's body dropped to the floor. Maddy screamed and grabbed onto Hunt and he held her while the soldiers closed in. The tall African walked to where Delvin's body lay and picked up the chrome Smith & Wesson.

"Just like Gentry's," he said, and felt the weight of it in his hand.

CHAPTER TWENTY-TWO

"I am Sergeant Bunting," the tall African said in a rounded accent. He stood in front of the group next to Delvin's contorted corpse. He held the Smith & Wesson 500 cradled in both palms. "You are prisoner's of McArthur Gentry and the Lord's Revelation Front."

Hunt held Maddy and she was shaking.

"Don't worry, everything will be alright," he whispered.

A group of blank faced soldiers stood behind Bunting in an arc, concealed by the trees, and watched. Others went past them towards the camp site.

VD rubbed the back of his head, "And the hits just keep on coming ... and bloody well say TIA."

Hunt looked around the group and they looked afraid.

"They're going to find the body," Fabrice said. He looked alarmed and was beaded with sweat. On cue there was a shout from the camp and a howl of frustration. Bunting's eyes were locked on Hunt's. His eyes narrowed and his lips were pursed. He waited for the men to come back with what they'd found. One carried Michael's limp, dead body over his shoulder and flopped it down next to Delvin like a bag of flour. The stench of death was immediate and overwhelming.

Maddy gagged. Insects crawled out of the cavities in Michael's face. Bunting continued to stare. He didn't seem angry, he seemed calm and blank. Slowly, he turned and gave his men instructions. Others arrived carrying the day sacks and provisions.

Bunting directed a small detachment to stay and bury the bodies. To the others, he indicated that they would be moving out shortly. A couple of soldiers came and used zip-ties to secure each of the remaining expeditions' hands behind their backs. They were rough and pulled the ties tight. Hunt didn't blame them with their comrade lying dead to their front, his pale face eaten away by bugs.

One of the soldiers grabbed the satellite phone from Hunt's hand and presented it to Bunting. He shook it gently in acknowledgement to Hunt and gave the order to move out. His men fell in behind and they pushed and shoved the expedition into line and they left that place of death.

HUNT WATCHED the soldiers around them. They were small and exceptionally dark skinned. They had high protruding cheek bones and stared blankly. No talking or singing. They were well drilled and obedient. He compared it with the expedition team. He felt weak. The venom laid waste to his muscles and energy levels. His body was still recovering. VD nearly died. Hunt saw him occasionally touch his throat and windpipe. His eyes looked sunken and he had burst blood vessels and early signs of bruising around the collar of his shirt. Maddy looked like she was in shock. She looked at the ground and muttered to herself. Fabrice was behind Stirling, he loped along, but stumbled occasionally and found it hard to walk with his wrists strapped behind his back. He'd tried to converse, but the soldiers around him quickly shut him down and threatened him with the butts of their AK-47s.

The gloom of the jungle made the going difficult as they marched through rotting leaves and rancid mud.

"I can't believe Delvin," Maddy said under her breath.

Hunt glanced at her, "I know."

"What was he talking about? MI6?"

"I don't know," Hunt said. He lied. And watched Maddy out the corner of his eye.

"No talking," one of the soldiers barked.

Sergeant Bunting signalled back and one of the young soldiers bringing up the rear, jogged past Hunt and Maddy and ran to the front of the column. Bunting spoke to the boy and he nodded once and set off running ahead of the group. They must not have been far away from where they were going if Bunting was sending runners to warn of their arrival, Hunt thought.

"We can't be far now," Hunt said to Maddy. Later they came to the river and followed the bank. The same clearing where Hunt had first encountered Bunting came into view. He looked up and lifted his hand to his face and shielded it against the glare. The mountain stood tall and cone-shaped and green off to his right. The mud turned to sand and became soft underfoot and the column struggled to walk through it. Maddy slipped and stumbled. Hunt caught her. Her lips were cracked and she was pale.

"We need water," Hunt said to the guards.

"Keep moving," was the only reply.

They left the sand behind and walked into the gloom and depth of the forest again. It was cool and their clothes were heavy with sweat. Hunt knew if they didn't stop or get water soon, he would lose the team to thirst and disease.

THE EXPEDITION STUMBLED ONWARD. They were afraid of their fate. The soldiers pulled them forward, eager to get home. After hours of marching through the jungle they found a well trodden path and the canopy changed and opened. They headed downward, on a shallow gradient. Hunt was aware of other soldiers in the tree line. They joined the column and jeered at the prisoners and jabbered to their colleagues excitedly.

"Where are we going?" Maddy said to Hunt and looked up at him. She was afraid and in shock.

"Listen, there is something I need to tell you," Hunt said.

"Don't, please," she begged, "I don't want to know anymore."

"It's important," Hunt said, "it's about what Delvin was talking about."

She shook her head and bit her lip, "Please don't. No more."

Hunt faced front and kept quiet. She needed to hear the truth. The lie was unraveling faster than he could control it.

"We're all going to die," she said, "And I am going to get the worst of it."

Fabrice overheard and tried to comfort her, but a soldier smacked him with the butt of his rifle and he relented and let her alone. As they walked the landscape changed. It seemed more managed, more manicured. The ground was a carpet of brown leaves. They seemed placed. There were tracks running into the forest and bush and foliage seemed tended to.

"Did you notice where we've walked?" Hunt asked her.

She shook her head.

"The mountain is behind us. We're on its north westerly slope. The down gradient. Ring any bells?"

He could see her thinking, turning it over her head. She became more alert. More aware, and it lifted her morale.

"The satellite images," she said, "was I right?"

CHAPTER TWENTY-THREE

The more they went downhill, and the closer they seemed to their destination, the more aggressive and restive the soldiers became. Hunt saw huts and bomas concealed in the trees. Then, the trees gave way, and the land opened in front of them. They stood on a wide rock outcrop. The rock was a dry tan and white in places. The forest was held back by the insoluble rock. The high, swaying trees seemed to lean, as if trying to get a view of what was going on in the quarry below.

The soldiers grabbed and pushed them and yelled. They were hustled down a rock path and led into the quarry below. The scene was surreal and captivating and strange. After hours traipsing through uneven, muddy, insect infested rainforest canopy with no view of the sky, this was like an oasis. The trees banked up like tower blocks in a city and the sky was a circle of warm blue. It was cool in the shade of the trees and the light hurt their eyes. They looked unwashed, unrested and unhealthy. Hunt was pushed forward to the front of the group of assembled soldiers. The others were with him. And Bunting was at the head. The soldiers in front of them parted and Hunt saw a man standing on a carved white stone table. He had his hands on his hips and a black beret tucked under the shoulder epaulette of his olive green fatigues.

"My soldiers," the man bellowed and raised his arms, "Mlondolozi!"

The soldiers around them raised the fists and echoed, "*Mlondolozi!*"

"God be with you," the man on the table said.

"And also with you," they replied in unison.

"We have a great victory!" he enthused, and a deep-bass hum rumbled through the assembly.

"We have a sign from God!" And he looked to the sky and pointed, "And, we have our enemy in our church," he glared at Hunt and the others and the bass-like rumble continued and the faces turned to the prisoners.

"Who is that?" Maddy whispered.

"McArthur Gentry," Hunt said without looking at her. He felt her watching his face. Possibly wondering how he knew, or who McArthur Gentry was.

Gentry hopped down from the table. The bass-like hum continued and as he walked towards Hunt, the soldiers around them spread out like flames in a field and then left. Sergeant Bunting fell in beside Gentry and he walked up to inspect the prisoners.

"We killed one in the jungle," Bunting said, as Gentry looked up at Hunt and studied him. Gentry moved to inspect Maddy and did so like a General assessing his troops on a parade ground.

"They killed one of our men," Bunting said, and Gentry turned to look at him.

"We shall have to have a funeral ceremony for our fallen comrade, Sergeant," Gentry said.

"Yes, sir."

"See to it please," Gentry said, and turned back to his new prisoners, "which one of you killed him, I wonder?"

He turned on his heels. The expedition stood silently in a line.

"Was it you little miss straw-in-your-hair?" Maddy quivered and looked away. "Was it the giant coconut?" Gentry asked, meaning Fabrice. "Or, perhaps, this white devil here, *hmm*?" Gentry turned the inside of Hunt's arm and observed the bite mark on the crease of his arm.

"Which was it?" Gentry asked and turned to look at Bunting.

"You killed him in the forest," Hunt said, "you have your retribution."

Gentry stood still and looked at Bunting for a long moment.

"Who is this man, who talks to me, as if I needed his advice?" he asked, his voice rising to a shout at the end. Gentry turned and stood under Hunt's nose and spoke to him with specks of spit hitting his chest.

"Our God is a God of vengeance. An eye for an eye, a tooth for a tooth. We will have a sacrifice and a funeral for our comrades and you will provide the leverage we need." Gentry turned to Bunting, "Put him in the pit."

Bunting signalled to two soldiers and they came and grabbed Hunt roughly by the arms and led him away.

"No!" Maddy cried and then bit her lip and hid her face. Gentry glared, but said nothing.

VD and Fabrice watched Hunt being led away, and he shouted back, "Don't let them get to you. Don't tell them anything!"

One of the soldiers hit Hunt across the jaw and Hunt used his strength to stop walking and turned to face the man who'd hit him. His eyes studied the face. He made a mental note. The soldier looked away and Hunt let them push him towards his sentence. As they walked he looked at the rising stone walls of the quarry. There were caves and carvings cut into the rock. A large central statue was carved into the rock. It had bulging eyes and a cone-shaped pointed hat. It glared out and the eyes seemed to follow as he moved.

They came to the far wall of the quarry. This part was darkly shaded by the trees and the rock wall overhung a long, narrow crack in the ground. In the middle of the crack was a hole, like a well for water, it was a midnight-black crevice. Hunt struggled against the grip and tried to turn. Everything inside him was telling him not to get in the pit. Death would be better than whatever lurked in the black hole.

"Get in," one of the guards said.

"No," Hunt said and struggled against their grip.

They struggled against him and forced him forward toward the hole. He resisted. His boots skidded on the smooth dust on the rock. He leaned against them and they grunted at the effort until he felt the momentum tip and he went into the hole. He tucked his chin. He fell into the abyss. No idea how deep or how far it was. His shoulder and face bounced off the rock wall. He tumbled into the darkness, winded and in pain, and hit a hard flat bottom. His face hit the stone floor and his mind disconnected like flicking a light switch and he was knocked out.

———

VD WATCHED as they dragged Hunt away. He had the sensation that he was observing himself from somewhere above. He was very aware that he'd nearly died. He'd seen a vision. He'd been hurtling down a long white tunnel and people from his life, those he'd hurt, those he'd loved, and those he'd wished he could have seen again, were on the outside of the tunnel, watching him. Then he'd taken a sudden, life affirming breath in, and seen his friend. He knew he'd been close to never coming back. The afterglow of the chemical shock to his brain was a buddhist-like calm. He observed

Gentry as a curiosity, but he was afraid for Maddy and Fabrice.

"How many crates were you carrying aboard your flight?" Gentry asked and VD snapped back to the present.

"How many," Gentry said again.

VD inadvertently shook his head, he couldn't remember the manifest. A lot.

"We believe we have most of them," Bunting said.

"What are you doing here? In Equatorial Varrissa," Gentry asked.

"Geological survey," Maddy said. Her voice was dry and raspy and she cleared her throat.

Gentry laughed.

"No, you're here to assassinate me. Don't lie. The god of these walls sees all," and he tutted. "You have much equipment, you must show me how to use it. We will make a call to your colleagues in London. I require a decent satellite communications system in order to negotiate a price."

"What price?" Maddy asked, defiant.

"Why, for you my dear, and my other guests. I am sure his mother must be worried sick. Close to tears."

"You killed the only man who could build that array," she said, and then quickly added, "And the other, you've just thrown in a pit."

"Ah, I think you must think you are very smart," Gentry said and wagged his index finger at her with a wry look on his face, "and you must think me very stupid. You think I am a chimpanzee Miss ...?"

"Chasm," she said.

Gentry looked at Bunting and nodded and dropped his lower lip, impressed.

"No," Gentry said, "Miss Chasm, you will help us construct the array, when asked, for now you can rest, as my guests. Sergeant, take them away. And put this one to work," he said, meaning Fabrice.

Maddy and VD were led away and turned to look back at Fabrice standing forlorn in a white stone quarry of emptiness and fear. A single tear ran down his cheek as Maddy and VD looked back and tried to think of something to say, but nothing came. They were led out of the quarry and back into the forest. VD jostled with the guards.

"Relax," the one guiding them said, "you will see your friends."

They ducked under a low thatched roof and in the gloom saw floor to ceiling wooden cages. There were two bodies in one of the cages. They looked thin and dirty and barely looked up when they entered. VD kept watching them as they were led into a wooden cage next to the two men. The longer, thinner prisoner of the two lifted his hand in a greeting. The guard locked their cage and VD sank to the floor.

CHAPTER TWENTY-FOUR

Hunt groaned. He lay on his side with his cheek against a cold, stone surface. He rolled and felt the pain in his shoulder and neck from the fall. It was completely dark in the pit. He moved his feet to try and feel around in the dark. Try and gauge the size and shape of the hole. The air was musty. The floor felt cold and damp under his palms. He lay on them and they felt swollen and hard to move, like gloves that were too small.

He felt despair. Alone in the dark. No idea how deep his prison cell was. And no idea what happened to the team. He rolled onto his stomach and got to his knees. He closed his eyes. He had the same amount of vision with them closed or with them open. Hunt pushed his concentration to his other senses. He listened. There were distant, low sounds, he tried to imagine the shape of the pit. Was it man-made? Or a natural crack in the earth?

He shuffled forward and felt the cold radiating off the rock face. He moved up to it and turned his cheek. It felt smooth. Possibly man-made. Built as a prison?

He turned and felt along it with his hands. He looked for a sharp or jagged edge with his fingers. His fingers brushed the surface lightly and felt around as best he could for a place to saw his zip-tied wrists free. He shuffled slowly backwards and came to an edge, or corner of the pit. It wasn't round like a well, but he thought, more narrow, like a cat's pupil. He turned back on himself and shuffled. His feet touched something and he stopped, reached back and his finger's climbed the wall, searching. He felt something hard and dry. It was cold, but felt different to the stone walls. It moved and cracked and he realised what it was. His hands were feeling up a human skull. He jumped in fright and felt a twinge up his spine, like a large spider was crawling over him in the dark. He jumped forward and fell onto the cold stone floor. This was hopeless. He was going to die here. Was Gentry just softening him up for supper? Waiting for him to weaken so he might welcome his fate?

It was hopeless. He lay there in darkness, and breathed the fine dust on the stone floor of the dark crevice, at the bottom of a dark hole, cut into the earth by blood and sweat and metal, into the side of a dark corner, of a dark country, in the beating heart of darkness.

CHAPTER TWENTY-FIVE

It started to rain. The air grew thick and heavy. It made it hard to breathe. The pressure built, and then, like a sluice, the water came down. Hunt heard the rolling thunder and then the cracks of lightning. The white streaks struck the trees and hard ground around them. The flash after flash lit the pit like a strobe. He'd only experienced a storm like that once before. The large lake in the mountains of their ranch in Zimbabwe attracted bolts of lightning like a temple to Zeus.

Hunt stood and looked up and out of the crack at the entrance to his crevice. The lightning sparked a glow and dazzled his eyes; he saw the jagged fracture in the rock above him. It was out of his reach and just overhead. He put his arms up and test jumped, but it was too high. And the rain came down. The sound rose like waves crashing on a rocky shore. Slow at first and then loud and consistent. A wall of white noise.

Hunt knew he had no time. Only for as long as the rain lasted, would no-one move. Every man and every animal would seek shelter and wait out the explosive anger of the god of thunder. He stood listening to the rain and watched for the light. He wondered if the mission was a setup. If someone betrayed them. Someone used his connection to Digger and his drive to protect against him.

Hunt looked to the corner and at the corpse. The next flash of lighting showed a mummified skeleton. Ragged clothes hung off the bones and the face still had folds of dried skin and tufts of dry hair. It was time to do something. He walked over to the corpse. It grinned at him with the maniacal face of a jaw without lips, but still with rows of brown and blackened teeth.

"Now, don't go losing your head," he said to himself, as much as to his silent roommate. He hunched down and felt for the jaw, and wriggled his fingers until they were underneath the skull, and twisted. The head twisted away from the spine and it crackled and popped and tore loose. He used his teeth to untie his boots and used his feet to remove them, one after the other. Then lay on his back and arched it. He slid his hands to his buttocks and cried out at the pain and slipped his forearms down the back of his legs and free. His muscles screamed out at the stress. He lay and panted for a moment. His arms were in front of his body.

He grabbed the skull and held it between his feet like a coconut and twisted it so that the row of upper teeth faced him.

"Have you been flossing?" he asked and smiled and put the plastic from the zip tie against the incisors. He moved his hands up and down along them like he was planing wood. He felt the skull bend and the teeth loosen as he built up the friction. The crunch and churn of the dried skull felt sickening. As he lost hope and began to tire the plastic cable tie snapped free.

"Ah, sweet relief," he said and tilted his head back and breathed. "How was it for you?" he asked the loose-toothed skull and grinned. He massaged his hands and rubbed the skin where the sharp plastic bit. Rain ran in through the slit in the ceiling. He saw the shine of the water flowing like a flat waterfall, but it wasn't collecting in the bottom. There was a runoff somewhere. He went where the skeleton lay. Its clothes sagged and stank. He patted it down and felt in its pockets.

"Anything useful in here?" he asked and looked back at the skull. There was some change in the pockets, it felt and smelled like old copper coins. He felt around the back and patted it down, his face closer to the bones than he would ever have wished. He felt something in the back pocket, a bulge. He stuffed his hand down and pulled out a piece of cloth.

"Disappointing, I thought it might be something good," he said. He felt something hard and rectangular wrapped in the cloth. He pulled it out and held it up during a flash of lightning. A cigarette lighter. Small and plastic. He shook it next to his ear. It sounded like there was still some juice in it, but not much.

"Bless you, you poor bastard," he said, and stopped just short of giving the skull a kiss on the forehead.

CHAPTER TWENTY-SIX

Hunt sat alone in the dark. The rain pelted down outside. The bright lightning skies had passed. He twirled the lighter in his fingers and thought. He was afraid to try it. What if it didn't work? Or, what if it worked ... what would he do then anyway?

He watched the water rush in, slip over the edge of the opening, and slide down the smooth crevice wall. He checked his feet, they weren't wet. The water wasn't collecting in the bottom. He wouldn't drown at least.

Where was it going?

He got up and walked to the wall below the sliced opening above his head and put his hand on the cold, grey rock. He slid his hand down to the ground and felt along it. He moved into a dark corner, opposite the skeleton. Suddenly his hand slipped into the darkness. There was another crevice. He decided to try the lighter. One blast of light, just enough to get an idea of what he was looking at. He flicked the flint. It sparked, but no flame. He tried again and again. The sweet sound of *schlick-shhh* and he had a flame. He had a dopey grin on his face and moved the flame along the darkness. He could see a rectangular gap, like a letterbox, along the floor. He cut the light and put it away. The risk was, if he went down there, he wasn't sure he would ever get out. He reasoned with it for some time.

If they planned on pulling him out of here in future, surely they would pull him out of the next cavern? If they planned to let him rot, like his friend there, what difference did it make? He sat for a long time and stared at the letterbox slot. He couldn't see it, but he knew it was there. The idea built in his mind.

"Screw it," he said and stood again. "Sorry, chum." He yanked off the skeleton's arm and took it to the slot. Here goes nothing, and threw it into the blackness. It didn't fall and bounce, it sounded more like it slid. There wasn't a steep drop, just a gradient that ran away from him. That was interesting. He undressed the skeleton.

"Don't get any ideas," he said as he pulled the trousers off. He tied everything together and then looped it all around a femur, fibula and tibia. He checked to make sure it was sturdy and then wedged the bones against the letterbox-slot. He checked his pockets to make sure he had the lighter and then eased himself to the floor and next to the slot. It was a tight squeeze. He exhaled and tried to collapse his ribcage and then got panicked and withdrew.

"Come on," he said to himself and got back down. This time he exhaled forcefully and wriggled and pulled until his torso popped through. It smelled damp and mouldy. His shirt was soaked with rain water and it felt cold. He heard the drip and running of water and slid belly first like a penguin towards the sea. He pulled himself forward and the ceiling narrowed and was sharp and he hit another wall. He fumbled around in the dark and had the sense that he wasn't alone. He twisted and pulled out the lighter. Said a silent prayer and flicked the flint. The flame sparked and he glimpsed a human skull smiling wide and vacant at him. He felt like a spider was crawling up his arm and shook it free. He knocked something behind him as he did and another pile of bones fell on his leg. He yelped and cried out, "*Ah! Aaaah!*"

He took a breath and calmed himself, "Get a grip," he said and flicked the flint again. This time the flame stayed and swayed with his breath. He had a quick look around. The water was still running out to somewhere, but he couldn't see any more openings. He was surrounded by corpses. Three decayed skeletons in loose fitting clothing. "A little too close for comfort fellas," he said and twisted to get more of the picture. He pushed the skeleton behind him and rolled onto something hard, looked down and saw the bones of the fingers clutched onto something.

He pulled it up by the wrist and saw it was a piece of stone. The old bones gripped it hard and he pried it loose and examined it. One side was flat and the same colour as the stone around him. The other protruded out, like the point of a pickaxe. He held it up to the light. The flat side looked like it was covered with a yellow moss. Like some golden organism was growing on it. And then he realised what he was looking at. Not a gold-looking organism. Gold. He twisted to see and shone the light along the rock face. The yellow flame danced against the face and a shimmer ran over the surface like the shine of a film of oil on water. Hunt put his hand up and pressed it against the reef. It was at least two hands thick, and who knew how long.

"She was right," he said. "She was right, boys!" He stuffed the nugget into his pocket. He knew he had to get out. And now he had a plan.

CHAPTER TWENTY-SEVEN

He tussled with the skeletons. They were all loose and flailing. He twisted his body in the tight space and pushed the corpses back up the slide. It was tough work and he kept losing purchase as his feet slipped on the wet slab. He felt above his head and found the end of the trousers on his escape rope. He held it and pulled the other skeletons up by their clothes, trying to keep them intact. He pulled them up and shoved them through the letterbox-slot at the top. He forced the last one through the gap and used his elbows and the clothes to pull himself at the top. He felt the bundle of bones slip.

"No, no, no," he gasped, and tried to pull himself to the top. He exerted a final force as the bone-anchor slipped and he lunged and managed to grab hold of the lip with his fingertips. He strained to curl his fingers over the lip and ease with his feet and knees without slipping. He dug his fingernails into the raised lip and gritted his teeth and shut his eyes against the pain and exertion. He got hold and managed to get his elbows out through the letterbox and dragged and crawled himself forward. He collapsed on his back and panted. He looked around at the four skeletons, "Welcome to the party," he said.

He got to his knees and got to work. He used the clothes to strap the skeletons together. He removed the skulls and piled them in the corner. He used the long leg bones to support the spines and tied it all together like it was Halloween. Each pelvis went on top of the spine and leg bones until he had an elongated pile of bones.

"This is never going to work," he said to the skulls on the wall. He positioned the bone ladder at the bottom of the crevice in the roof. It didn't look that far above him. He needed a good run up, a solid launch off the platform of bones, and to get enough of a grip at the top to pull himself through.

"You'll never know unless you go," he said with his back up against the wall. He ran at the opening like a power forward toward the net. He planted his foot against the step-ladder and drove upwards. His hands latched onto the crevice's lower lip. His legs kicked out and he knocked the bones to the side. He dangled and felt his fingers and fore-arms slipping back. He let himself go and dropped down into a hunch.

"Damn it." He had his head between his knees and breathed hard. He wondered how long he could keep this energy level up for. He tried again and again. It was no use. He couldn't get enough purchase on the ledge. It was still raining and the rock was slippery and smooth. He sat against the back wall and looked up at the hole in the sky. It was his escape. His only route to freedom. And it was too high. Unat-tainable.

He had an idea. He took his shirt off and wrapped it around his hands. He could use it to get more leverage, more grip. He stood up to try once more. And again he pressed himself to the back of the wall. He took some deep breaths.

He tensed his muscles like a sprinter in the blocks. As the starting gun was about to go, he thought he heard something. Voices. The rain was coming down as heavy as before and he strained against the noise. There it was again. Two voices. Were they coming his way? He crouched and pushed himself into the dark like an animal. He had his wet shirt in his hands.

Two heads covered with ponchos appeared at the crevice opening. Hunt looked up at them and saw them peering into the darkness below.

"Hey!" one of them called. "Prisoner, come now!"

Hunt was silent and pushed himself back into the corner. They spoke to one another. One of them leaned in and twisted his head to see further into the pit. Hunt saw the barrel of an AK-47 poke down. Then it withdrew and the man spoke to his colleague.

"Come, prisoner! We have food. Come and get food! We must throw it down."

Hunt stayed quiet. The head reappeared and looked in. The one out of sight handed the other something. A flashlight. The dull yellow beam shone into the darkness and Hunt closed his eyes and turned his head.

"Come now! We have food."

The one with the flashlight turned back to his colleague, ready to give up. Hunt lunged forward. The starter's gun went and his mind was clear and blank. He charged out of the blocks, planted his foot on the stepladder of bones, it crunched and broke underfoot. He saw the look of surprise on the man's face. He started to fall backward and Hunt lassoed his wet shirt around the barrel. He yanked and the man came forward. Hunt grabbed the barrel and pulled himself up. The man fell forward and Hunt clambered and clawed at his poncho and clothing. The man screamed. His colleague dropped the tray of food and it clattered and he scrambled to get away. There was a moment where Hunt was neither in the pit nor out, and his victim was suspended fighting the seesawing force. Hunt grabbed the man's trousers and pulled himself up. The soldier went face first into the darkness and Hunt landed on his haunches outside the crevice. He heard the snap as the soldier hit the stone floor below him in the darkness.

Hunt looked up through the rain. His hair was in his eyes and pressed flat against his brow. He saw the other soldier on all fours cycling backwards. His eyes were wide and afraid. Hunt grabbed the metal tray off the floor. Apples were scattered on the ground and Hunt stepped through them and lifted the tray. Hunt swung it and the man raised his arms and screamed. A single, piercing shriek made it out of his throat before the edge of the metal caught him in the temple and his body sagged. Hunt felt the anger surge and he brought the tray down again and again.

When he was done he had crimson blood specks sprayed up his torso. Raindrops ran into them and they turned pink and disappeared. He felt the fear and anger seep away. He realised how close he was to death. The stench of the bones and musk of the pit remained.

He sat on top of the corpse and breathed and looked around. The cold rain felt like a baptism. New life. The high walls of the quarry were around him. He couldn't see anyone else. He patted the body down and tried not to look at it's face. The wounds were deep slashes from ear to jaw, like it had been trapped in the blades of a combine harvester. He found a blade in a sheath and attached it to his belt, took the poncho off the dead body and put it on. He dragged the corpse to the opening and pushed it into the pit. He was hungry and cold and picked up an apple and bit into it. It was sour.

"They say you can't make apple pie without cracking a few eggs ..." and chucked the rest into the darkness after the bodies.

CHAPTER TWENTY-EIGHT

Hunt looked around. The rain created a curtain of mist and a low grey cloud hung over them. He saw no movement. He heard no shouts and no alarms. The vertical, jagged wall above the crevice looked down at him. He traced a line up through the sharp rocks. He knew he couldn't go up and out the way he'd been brought here. Too many caves and hideouts filled with too many of Gentry's rebels looking down over the quarry.

Hunt climbed. He used the poncho to keep the rain from his eyes and his shirt as a glove. It was slow going and his feet slipped often. He turned and looked back. The glistening rock looked far below him now. He kept expecting to hear shouts, or the sound of gunfire. Nothing came. He got to the top and heaved himself over the ledge and ran into the line of trees. His hands and body ached. His heart was beating fast and he was short of breath. The nylon on the poncho rubbed and made a swishing sound. He decided it was best to leave it. He buried it at the base of a tree. He tucked his shirt into the back of his trousers. It was soaked, but maybe good for later. He spent moments crouched, gathering himself, and slathered on layers of mud as camouflage. He inspected the dirt to make sure there were no black or red army ants, then rubbed it on like soap in the shower. He tucked the hunting knife in his waistband and set off.

Hunt boxed around the quarry. It was well guarded on all sides by primary jungle. Thick trees, easy going underfoot, and with many places to hide. The air was denser and warmer inside the tree line. Hunt would stop, watch, and listen. The mist and cloud seemed to be clearing. The rain was subsiding. He didn't have much time and felt that the encampment would be more lively soon. As he moved he noticed more sounds coming from the woods. The occasional hint of smoke or the smell of tobacco. No doubt whoever sent the men to feed him would be wondering where they were by now. He'd moved around the quarry to his left, heading west, it was more or less back towards where they had come from. He remembered seeing huts and low slung cabanas and well tended paths and tracks.

Where would I put my prisoners as a power hungry cannibal with a God complex? Near the entrance to my lair, far away from the temptation for prying eyes, and the first line of defence in case of a surprise attack from my enemies. Let them be the collateral damage. If Hunt knew Gentry like he thought he knew him, he knew where the prisoners would be. He moved through the jungle and it changed. It was secondary jungle now, thick, bamboo-like forest. Difficult underfoot and dense thick foliage. Signs of the old settlements. Places where the Lord's Revelation Front hid and hunkered down, before their next violent rampage against the simple people of the region.

Hunt moved forward. He saw a guard playing with a stick, drawing lines in the mud. He got down low so his belt buckle touched the cold, wet earth and dragged himself forward on his elbows. He was under a fern and looked across an opening towards an open walled gazebo-type structure. He peered in and thought he saw the white skin of dirty feet in the gloom.

He pulled the knife from his waistband and held it so the flat edge of the blade was against his wrist. Hunt held his breath and listened. He heard nothing dangerous. Drops dripping from the leaves. Birdsong. A cough from under the hut. Then a rage of a sneeze. The guard jumped and grabbed his rifle. Hunt knew that sound anywhere.

"*Jammer*," the apology came in Afrikaans from under the thatch.

Hunt waited for the guard to settle again. He was excited and his blood was up. He knew what he needed to do. When the guard was drawing in the mud once more, Hunt got into a crouch, like a jet black jaguar, and stole forward. His foot squelched in the mud and the guard looked up, but it was too late. Hunt's forearm was across his mouth. He plunged the blade into the soft tissue behind the windpipe and twisted. Hunt held his arm across the enemy's mouth and withdrew the blade. A long looping spray of blood jumped from the carotid artery. Hunt put his hand over the soldier's eyes. The guard resisted, but Hunt knew he'd be unconscious within seconds, and dead in minutes. Hunt heard shushing and activity under the thatch of the gazebo. He checked the path left and right, picked up the AK-47 lying at the guard's feet, and dragged the limp body under the shelter.

He heard a gasp from Maddy and saw VD put his hand across her mouth. He shook his head and put his index finger to his mouth. Hunt left the body and went over to the cage with Digger and Lord Langdon. They looked weak.

"I don't believe it," Digger said. His face was dirty and etched with lines. Hunt put his hand through the bars.

"We'll get you out of here."

"Good man," Langdon said. He was weak, but excited.

Hunt twisted his head and listened. He heard men shouting. Their voices approached. He moved fast.

"Quick, get out of here," Digger hissed.

Hunt went back to the body.

"Here, take this," he whispered to VD and handed him the blade in its sheath. VD put it away. Hunt saw the horrified look on Maddy's face.

"I didn't want to do it," Hunt said quickly, "but I can't get you out unless I do."

The thump of footsteps approached. Hunt slung the rifle and dragged the body away from the hut and out of sight.

CHAPTER TWENTY-NINE

Hunt was in the undergrowth behind the prisoner's hut. He heard Gentry's soldiers giving orders and sending his soldiers in different directions. Searching for him, no doubt. His time was up. His luck was running out. He covered the guard's body as best he could with soil and rotten leaves and stopped to listen. There was commotion at the jail.

Hunt heard a strict, deep voice say, "Where is he?" and "Come with me."

He heard the locks clack open and the wooden gates crack. He got on his belt buckle again and leopard crawled deliberately forward. He had an angle through the undergrowth and caught a glimpse of Maddy struggling against the grip of Gentry's soldier. The others followed. VD stiff and upright. Digger and Langdon hunched and weak.

He had no time. Gentry was planning something. It was blend in, or get found out. Hunt decided the shallower northern side of the quarry would be best. It overlooked the courtyard area where they'd been inspected on arrival as 'Gentry's guests'. But, it was a risk. He'd have to cross the jungle footpath in front of the prison hut again. Hunt decided to head deeper into the jungle. He'd box around the position and cross the path further away. Less possibility of one of Gentry's men seeing him. He could hear the noise and activity of a company of men mobilising. Shouts. Sections of men moving together. They were searching for him.

There was no rain to cover his movement. He moved, crouching low and with haste.

HE BOXED around the position and moved through the secondary jungle. It was hard going and slow. The jungle turned again to primary forest. The undergrowth opened up and the trees turned to giants and loomed overhead. He knew he was on the northern side and turned at a right angle to head back to the quarry. Hunt crawled forward. He kept low and cradled the rifle in his arms and pulled himself towards the target.

His view of the entrance hall was wide and clear. Soldiers moved up and down the banked entrance to the subterranean fortress. He looked down on the giant stone table and the fire pit. Gentry's corporals and sergeants gave their men orders and pointed in different directions.

Then Hunt saw the prisoners. Maddy was still in the lead, pushed forward by a burly black man. The others followed. There was a sharp burst of activity. Soldier's straightened up and the junior ranks hurried about. Hunt saw why. Gentry made his way, followed by a small entourage, to the stone slab table.

Hunt saw something else. A hulking figure shuffling along behind Gentry. He was in manacles, head bowed and looked tired. It was Fabrice. He was downcast, his face swollen. He looked like a circus elephant. Chained, with sad eyes.

Hunt watched and waited. He knew groups of soldiers were out looking for him. He tried to think like Gentry. How would a maniacal psychopath react?

GENTRY WALKED UP to the line of prisoners. They looked like a group awaiting a firing squad. Fabrice followed close behind. Hands clasped, head bowed. He was defeated. Gentry paced. Maddy, VD and Digger were shoulder to shoulder. Langdon slouched and weak. Armed guards stood behind them. Gentry was speaking. Hunt could see his lips moving, but he couldn't hear the words. He brought the AK-47 up slowly and deliberately. He was well concealed, and knew he was within the effective range of the rifle. The problem was, how well had the weapon been maintained. It was old and he wasn't confident.

His feet were spread and he put his cheek into the stock and looked down the iron sights. He was on a downward slope and at a right angle to Gentry. The AK-47 had a long, curved magazine that Hunt rested on the soft soil. It meant his prone firing position was raised and he was more exposed. He concentrated on his breathing. The sight lifted and sank with each breath. It was deliberate and measured. He felt comfortable. His mind zoned in on the target.

Gentry was close to the line of prisoners, pacing under their noses. He was goading them. Spitting bile at them like a Sergeant Major on the Parade Square. Pure intimidation. Hunt felt good to know a bullet would soon be lodged in Gentry's malformed grey matter.

"*Move*, goddamn you," Hunt implored.

He wanted Gentry to step back. Give him the shot. AK-47 rifles lose accuracy with age, and they weren't the most accurate to begin with. Not for this type of precision work. It was like a brain surgeon operating with a meat cleaver. The wrong tool for the job. Hunt watched. His vision was trained on Gentry. He stepped right up to Maddy. He was under her face. She was scared and trying to look away. The guard behind her grabbed a handful of her hair and her face upwards. Hunt twitched.

Gentry grabbed the back of her head and pulled her over to the stone-slab table. She stumbled as he jerked her violently. Gentry stepped up and stood on the table and moved her around by her long hair. Hunt could see the pain etched on her face. He had Gentry in his sights. His heart was beating rapidly. His breaths were shallow. He knew he could end it all right here. Complete objective one of the mission: kill McArthur Gentry. But, could he get Langdon out?

Gentry started to shout. The voice carried to Hunt and echoed off the rocks.

"I know you are out there," Gentry yelled. "You've sacrificed the lives of your comrades. They will die for what you have done. Hear me! Do you hear me? They are going to die ..."

Hunt believed him.

Gentry caught his breath and stared at the lip of the quarry, and scanned for Hunt. Gentry acted like he knew he was out there, watching. Hunt felt like Gentry could see into his soul. He was tired. Covered in mud and rotten leaves. He was cold. And he had to make a decision about whether to exert a concentrated amount of pressure on a small metal lever and fire a copper-plated steel jacket projectile into the chest of one of the worst mass murderers Africa had ever seen.

"Give yourself up now!" Gentry screamed.

He reached into the back of his trousers and pulled out a chrome Magnum .44 and pressed the barrel against Maddy's temple. The long barrel made him stick his elbow out to his side like a teapot. Now was the time. If Hunt was going to press the trigger, now was the time.

"I am going to count to three," Gentry shouted. Maddy was crying. VD and Digger turned their heads. Lord Langdon stared out from under his eyebrows, mouth wide. The other soldiers simply watched and kept following Gentry's eyes to see where he was looking. Hunt was sure that Gentry knew where he was. He must. Otherwise, how could be so brazen, so confident, so unhinged?

"One," Gentry said, and pulled the hammer back. "Two."

CHAPTER THIRTY

"Stop!" Hunt yelled and jumped to his feet. He had the rifle above head.

"Stop, stop! Here I am. I'm here."

Gentry's eyes scanned for the source of the sound. He pushed Maddy forward and released her. She fell onto her knees and sobbed. Hunt dropped the rifle and kept his hands above his head. Bunting barked orders and soldiers came running. Gentry stood with his hands on his hip and grinned. Hunt could see the white teeth shining through the dark mask. He looked down at VD and Digger and they looked back at him. Hunt shook his head. He felt it was over.

Two young looking soldiers broke through the under-growth and walked up to him aggressively. One stared at Hunt and gritted his teeth. The soldier bent and picked up Hunt's rifle. He breathed through his nose and flared his nostrils and smashed Hunt in the gut with the rifle. It knocked the wind out of him and he doubled over coughing.

HUNT WAS FORCED BACK into the quarry. They kicked him down the slope and he fell and rolled. The others were lined up with backs against the quarry wall. The soldiers picked Hunt up and forced him down at the edge of the line, next to VD. Hunt looked across at them. One of the soldiers guarding them shouted, "Face the front. Shut your mouth." They didn't speak. Hunt sat watching Fabrice. He wouldn't make eye contact.

Gentry had gone. Bunting was the focal point of attention. The soldiers scurried back and forth like ants getting directions from the queen. Bunting was an impressive figure. Calm, focused and had the air of confidence that earned respect. Bunting reminded Hunt of Digger. He looked over at his old brother-in-arms. In his prime he was a formidable fighter and leader. He looked in bad shape. The whole team was on their last legs.

The soldiers were busy. It looked like they were setting up for a party. Hunt noticed pairs of soldiers running out with square yellow boxes. They were scuffed and dirty, but they'd managed to find and collect most of the containers Hunt had pushed out of the downed Fokker-50. Bunting moved along the line of containers and popped their lids. He called Fabrice over and spoke to him quietly. They looked to be discussing the contents. Fabrice nodded along solemnly. He looked ashamed.

The sun faded and the night drew in. Maddy shivered against the cold. Hunt felt naked and exposed and pulled his wet shirt out of his back pocket. The guard panicked at the movement and screamed at him to stop. He lifted his hands and tried to explain, but the guard hit him square in the face with the butt of his rifle and kicked him in the torso.

"Stop it!" Maddy screamed and dived on top of Hunt. She put her palm up at the guard as he swung his boot back.

"Halt!" Bunting boomed. The guard stopped his follow through before his toe-cap smashed into Maddy's face.

Bunting marched over and berated the soldier.

"Leave him be, Sergeant," Gentry's voice came out of the darkness. Soldiers to his side lit the bonfire. The flames shot up in the stone-walled pit and the yellow glow hit his face. Bunting turned to face Gentry and the soldier smirked. Hunt saw Bunting's face harden. His jaw was locked and lips pursed. Not impressed with Gentry for undermining him.

"These people are the enemies of God. Lower than the dogs. Tonight, we will make a sacrifice to the god of this place. We shall drink their blood. And you will know my name is the Lord when I lay my vengeance upon thee," Gentry said and glared at the prisoners.

"Where is my dog?" Gentry asked.

Fabrice came shuffling out of the shadows and stood with bowed head at Gentry's shoulder.

"Which one of these devils can build the satellite system?" Gentry asked and waved a hand at the prisoners.

"The woman," he said softly.

Gentry lifted his chin and the soldier turned and lifted Maddy off of Hunt's body.

"I'm sorry," she whispered as she stepped away.

Maddy and Fabrice started pulling out components from the yellow transport boxes. They spoke softly to one another. Hunt sat up. Maddy put her hand on his arm. He flinched and moved away.

Hunt was left alone with VD, Digger and a fading Lord Langdon.

"Gentry," Hunt called. "What are you going to do when Lord Langdon dies from exposure or malnutrition? What are you going to do then?"

The guard lifted his rifle to beat him. Hunt didn't flinch. Gentry started to laugh. A low rumble at first. The soldier looked back and lowered the weapon. Gentry's laugh built. The other soldiers joined in. The laugher rumbled out into the darkness, like the thunder before the rains. It rolled through the caves and crevices and turned into a murderous chorus.

THE NIGHT TURNED into a drug and alcohol fuelled party. Gentry sat at the head of the stone slab table. His company of child soldiers were below him. It was dark now. His soldiers were made up of all sorts. They were very young, some crossdressed and wore earrings and make up. They danced to west African rap, inspired by war, limb amputations, and killing their enemies. He looked down on them in the quarry like a school principal looked down from the stage at an assembly. Lord Langdon sat next to Gentry. His head wobbled. He looked dead on his seat. Gentry spoke to Langdon. He smiled and pointed to the soldiers dancing and drinking and shooting heroin below them. He laughed and slapped Lord Langdon on the shoulder like they were old friends swapping stories. Hunt couldn't hear what they were saying. When Gentry noticed him looking, the smile dropped from his face. Bunting, who was never far away, was summoned. Gentry spoke in his ear and Bunting walked up to Hunt.

"Come with me," he said and lifted Hunt by the armpit.

He guided him to the end of the table and placed him opposite Gentry. Gentry sat side on and rubbed his whiskers like he was stroking a cat. He glanced at Hunt and at his small army as they danced and drank. Hunt glanced over his shoulder. The armed guard stood behind him.

"This is a LRF funeral celebration, Mister Hunt," Gentry said.

He glanced at Langdon who was slumped and weak. The LRF were infamous for cutting off the limbs of the local populations who didn't support the guerrilla war they fought against Debby Mabosongo. They'd set up a stall and make judgements from a collapsable table, and at a nearby tree stump or a block of concrete they'd carry out sentencing, and amputate limbs. They would chop off innocent people's hands and forearms with an axe, or a cleaver, as punishment. They were also known for cutting out the hearts and livers of their enemies and feasting on them. Some of the soldiers, young boys, brainwashed with drink and drugs and power, said they loved the taste. Human flesh was their delicacy. It gave them power to carry out their holy mission and establish a garden of eden in Varrissa.

"Tell me, how did he die?" Gentry asked Hunt. Hunt knew he meant Michael, their former captive. He thought for a moment and said, "Honourably. He was murdered by a traitor from our expedition."

"And what is it you think you are doing here, in Equatorial Varrissa?" Gentry asked, taking an interest. He was softly spoken and earnest when it suited him. Hunt knew he could flick a switch and change the tone. He assumed a man bent on genocide, a well-known cannibal, would be unstable.

"We're on a research expedition," Hunt replied.

Gentry spun to face him and folded his hands, like it was a conference.

"Don't lie to me, Mister Hunt ... You will tell me everything I want to know."

Hunt nodded. He heard Maddy scream and looked up.

"Never mind that, they won't hurt her," Gentry waved his concerned look away. "They are only making sure she is ready for the big ceremony. Such a pretty, *tasty*, young thing, wouldn't you say?"

Hunt glared at him and Gentry smiled.

"Dog!" Gentry called and Fabrice stood up from assembling the communications station. He shuffled over to Gentry.

"Aren't you happy to see me, dog?" Gentry asked.

"I am boss," Fabrice said forlornly.

"Then wag your tail like a good boy," Gentry said, and Bunting smiled. Hunt was embarrassed. Fabrice shook his bottom and his body moved from side to side. The chains on his manacles jingled. He stuck out his tongue and panted and whined.

"Good boy," Gentry said. "How far is my machine?"

"Nearly finished." Fabrice stopped wagging.

"Go then," Gentry waved him away.

Hunt wondered what they must have done to emasculate someone like Fabrice. To make him act that way. He wondered what Gentry had in store for the rest of them.

"What is your plan, Mister Gentry?"

Hunt was direct. Gentry glanced at Bunting and he stepped forward.

"You are to address Supreme Commander Gentry as 'Lordship'," Bunting instructed. Hunt bowed his head and said, " ... Lordship."

"Why, to spark an invasion, Mister Hunt," Gentry answered. He must have seen the surprise on Hunt's face and leaned forward. "My demands are simple, the British government, the great colonial power of this land, will topple that corrupt dictator," he spat, "and install me as the rightful and one true power of this great nation."

"Why would they do that?"

"If they do not, I will rip out his heart and eat it live on their British Broadcasting Corporation," he said baring his teeth. He grabbed Langdon's shirt and yanked him forward. Gentry mimicked eating his heart.

"They'll never agree to that," Hunt said. He was unamused.

"Oh, yes? And how do you know? You're only on a research mission, aren't you?"

Hunt was quiet.

"Did you ever stop to ask yourself, how did *I* know where that fat idiot Koboko and this thin fool, Langdon, would be?"

Hunt didn't say anything. But he knew Gentry was right. How did Gentry know about the coup?

"You see? There is more than one puppet master pulling the strings," he turned and smiled and waved at his soldiers and clapped his hands. He was enjoying himself, for now. "Your British Government was happy to overthrow Dictator Debby and replace him with another, equally foolish dictator, so why not me? What's the matter with poor old me?"

Hunt saw the crazed look in Gentry's eyes. He grinned at Hunt without blinking.

"What are you going to do with the satellite link?" Hunt asked to change the subject.

Gentry waved the question away. "Issue my demands," he said.

"They'll never agree," Hunt said.

"Then your Lord Langdon will die." He turned from observing the party and looked back at Hunt. "I will kill a hostage every day until my demands are met. And after that, they will have to watch as Mabosongo executes the seventeen blood thirsty mercenaries that your Lord Langdon flew into the Republic to topple the regime and feed this country's riches to the oil companies of the world."

Hunt's jaw dropped. Seventeen private security contractors captured in the failed coup? If Digger was part of the planning of this, or at least supporting the Prime Minister's son, then Hunt might even know the soldiers behind bars. Hunt knew about torture. He saw his friends, brothers and fellow soldiers crammed in tight. Baking under the corrugated iron roofs and the unrelenting Varrissa sun. Fingers broken. Hands cuffed tightly behind their backs. Ankles in shackles. Boots stamping down on toenails and twisting as they rip them out. Their faces black and bodies bruised from the beatings. He couldn't bear the thought. He had to do something.

"Oh, you didn't know?" Gentry's shoulders shook up and

down as he laughed. Hunt turned and looked at Digger, he was sitting against the wall behind him. Digger nodded dejectedly, and Hunt turned back.

"Yes, Mister Hunt. I really must feel quite honoured that the British have sent you to assassinate me. And, quite amused in turn that they were willing to sacrifice seventeen of their own veteran soldiers to the gallows of Black Beach Prison, only to save this stinking wretch," he slapped a drowsy Langdon on the knee and rubbed it and laughed again.

"Oh, you look surprised," Gentry said. "Yes. Yes, your colleagues told me everything."

Hunt was sure he was bluffing, but couldn't be certain. Maddy and VD wouldn't say anything. Fabrice didn't know anything, did he? Delvin knew, but he was dead. Hunt's mind flicked through the possibilities like a deck of cards.

"It's nearly time for our sacrifice," Gentry said. He climbed onto the thick slab of stone. He held his arms aloft and his soldiers below turned and looked up and cheered. Hunt could see the looks on the boys faces below. Their eyes were glazed. They had goofy grins on their faces. The look in their eyes was as much one of fear as awe. A boy, no more than twelve, came up to Gentry and held up a torch. Gentry lit it. It burst to life like the Olympic torch. The crowd cheered. The young boy took off running. He ran around the amphitheatre-like walls of the quarry and held the flame to torches mounted into the stone. The yellow light bounced and flickered in the cool night. The crowd cheered and celebrated. Gentry quietened them.

"Tonight is a celebration of life!" he yelled out to them and they cheered. "Tonight is also about death," the crowd went quiet. "Tonight, the world will see the power of your Lord, beamed out to them by a global satellite. We will remember the brother we lost at the hands of these villains! These Satan worshipping devils, sent by our sworn enemy to kill your leader and the channel of your God!" The crowd bayed and hollered. Gentry quietened them again and they hushed.

"Bring out the sacrifice!" Gentry yelled and turned to look.

Hunt followed his gaze and saw Maddy coming out of the darkness in chains. She was stripped to her underwear. Held under her elbows by two guards. They carried her next to Gentry and the crowd went wild. They were blood-crazed, like a pack of hunting dogs chasing after a scent. She had tears rolling down her cheeks. Hunt's fist was tight under the table. He'd rather die.

He turned back and caught VD's eye. He gave him a nod and hoped VD understood. He saw VD reach into his boot and grab the handle of the hunting knife. The guard behind was watching the show, his rifle hung slack in his arms. Hunt waited for VD to make his move.

CHAPTER THIRTY-ONE

Gentry stood on the long, stone table and looked down at his assembled troops. The soldiers danced and partied and a few looked up at their leader. He lifted his arms and there was a sharp whistle and the music cut.

"Now, my soldiers," his voice echoed around the lower amphitheatre of the quarry. There was a nervous and excited tension in the air. "We have the main event. Just like The Binding of Isaac, on the site of Solomon's Temple, your Lord has commanded you to offer this sacrifice!"

A wild cheering broke out from the crowd below. Gentry beamed a smile and let the applause wash over him. He closed his eyes and tilted his head back, and beckoned them to keep it up. The roar grew louder, until he'd had enough and quietened them, and they hushed.

"These ... heathen!" he thrust his finger down at Hunt, "Have butchered one of our brethren." The crowd booed and hissed. "And so we too, like the Bible commands, shall take an eye for an eye, and tooth for a tooth!" They cheered wildly again. "They have sacrificed brother Michael to God, and so, we too shall sacrifice one of their own." The crowd bayed like hounds after a scent.

Gentry glanced back at Maddy. Hunt saw she was shaking, tears running down her face. Fabrice was helpless next to her.

"String her up!" Gentry commanded. The soldiers guarding her pushed forward a wooden frame. It had thick rope hanging down from each pole and footrests with manacles at the bottom. They planned to string her up in a spread-eagle, like a perverted crucifixion, where all of the soldiers could watch from the bottom.

"We will dance and celebrate and pray," Gentry said. "We will watch as God takes her life and then we will feast on her heart!" The crowd went into a frenzy. "Her brain!" They barked like a pack of dogs. "And her liver!"

The guards pulled her forward towards the platform and the ropes. She resisted, but she was no match. Hunt glanced back at VD. The soldier in front of VD glanced over his shoulder to see what Hunt was looking at. Hunt saw him turn his head, and at the same moment VD leapt up. He pulled the knife from his boot and drove it home. He pushed it deep into the soldier's neck. VD's momentum carried him and the guard forward and knocked into the man standing behind Hunt.

Digger charged. He knocked into the guard behind Hunt like an offensive lineman. The soldier was bowled forward. He fired his rifle on full automatic as he fell and the volley of rounds fired off and slammed into the rock face. There was panic in the ranks below and they screamed and crushed with the fright. Hunt saw Bunting unclip his pistol holster and go for the Magnum .44.

Hunt charged. As he drew, Hunt slapped his gun-hand to the side, in the same movement he pivoted. Hunt grabbed Bunting's arm and pinned it under his armpit. He bent the elbow back and rammed the back of his head into Bunting's face and forced him to the ground. Hunt had the handgun and wrapped his arm around Bunting's neck and lifted him from the floor. The other guards on the raised stage were yelling. Gentry pulled out Delvin's .50 calibre Magnum and dragged Maddy by the hair to stand in front of him.

"Don't move! Don't move!" Hunt yelled.

Bunting struggled and grunted, snot came out of his nose. Gentry pulled Maddy savagely to the side and crouched down behind her. He shouted to the soldiers down below, "Don't worry my brothers, this will all be over soon!"

There was silence, except for Bunting's grunting.

"My soldiers," Gentry said, addressing the two armed soldiers behind Hunt, "Listen to me now. I want you to shoot that white devil."

Hunt twisted his neck to see. The soldier's looked at one another. They looked uncertain, unsure.

"Yes, Lordship, but —"

"But, nothing!" Gentry screamed, "Do you dare question me?"

"No, sir, but —"

"What if they miss and hit you, Gentry?" Hunt was trying to buy some time. "Aren't you worried?"

Gentry moved slowly along the table in a crab-walk and dragged Maddy along by a fistful of hair. She shrieked and was dragged along.

"Now shoot him!" he screamed. He was desperate for control. Hunt had exposed him.

The soldiers behind looked at one another again. One lifted the rifle and aimed. His hands were shaking.

"Don't do it," Hunt said, "Sergeant Bunting dies if you pull that trigger."

The soldier hesitated again. He didn't know what to do. They both looked afraid. Gentry lost his mind. The demagogue in him broke loose. His veil of sanity slipped.

"I will kill this girl and eat her brain!" he screamed. "I am the Lord your God! Kill that traitor Bunting and kneel before me! Kill him now, in my name! I command you."

Hunt knew that Gentry had gone too far. Their leader

had exposed his true face, the mask had fallen. There was a shocked silence. The whole quarry was still, like a spell had been lifted. The soldiers' faces hardened.

Bunting spoke, "Commander Gentry has lost his mind. He has ordered you to kill me, but that is an evil spirit talking. The devil is inside of him. He has blasphemed and asked us to worship him as we would our one true Lord, the God above. We must relieve him of his duty," Bunting said. He was loud and solemn. The man they respected as a leader was there again. "Soldiers, remove the weapon from Commander Gentry's hands and disarm him."

The soldiers behind Hunt stepped forward. Gentry was backpedaling now. Maddy looked directly at Hunt. He mouthed, 'duck'. She gave a nod. Hunt let Bunting go and he fell forward. Maddy twisted and dropped. Her weight pulled her down. Gentry was exposed and Hunt took the shot. Gentry twisted. The bullet smashed into Gentry's shoulder and spun him around. He reeled backwards and collapsed. The thundering gunshot reverberated around the quarry. The moment, like a patient waking from hypnosis, was broken. Hunt shot the guards in front of him and turned the gun on Bunting. Bunting was on his knees and pleaded, "Please, don't shoot me please. You can go."

Soldiers from the lower levels started fighting to get up to the amphitheatre. The stairs were narrow and they bottlenecked, but some broke through. Hunt left Bunting on his knees and went to get Fabrice. He was in shock. Hunt grabbed a satellite phone from the setup and stuffed it in his trousers. He turned and saw VD cut Digger's wrists free. Digger picked up one of the discarded rifles and rounds thumped into the soldiers' as they stormed the stage. VD grabbed Langdon. He picked him up under the shoulders.

"Let's go!" Hunt yelled. They needed to fall back, get into the trees and escape. They had a Company of drunk, stoned child soldiers after them. Trust a person, but never trust a drug and there was no knowing what their drug-crazed minds would do with Gentry lying severely injured on the ground.

The whole team fell back. Hunt led Fabrice out. VD helped Maddy, and Digger carried Langdon under his armpit and fired the AK-47 from the hip.

"Keep moving," Hunt said. "They're mostly kids. Let's go."

"I know where the vehicles are," Digger yelled to Hunt as he passed.

"Lead the way," Hunt said.

THE EXPEDITION CHARGED into the darkness.

They followed the path past the cages. They grew quiet and moved fast through the jungle. It was hard going in the dark and they stumbled and fell. Langdon was struggling and Digger strained against his weight. Hunt saw Langdon's foot catch and he went down hard on his chest and face and groaned. Digger tried to lift him, "Come on, boss," he said.

"Wait, wait," Hunt said and let Fabrice walk by himself. "Let's regroup."

They stopped. They were in a sorry state, breathing hard and were tired and afraid. Then they heard a voice from the darkness, "White *karamapim tok*," it said.

Digger twisted and lifted his rifle.

"Wait, wait," Hunt said and stopped him. "I know that voice."

A twig snapped underfoot and the young pygmy hunter stepped out. He stood holding a long blowgun and leaned against it.

"It's you," Hunt said. "This man saved my life and VD's life too."

"I followed you," Batwa said. "I know where other white men are. Chief say, I take you 'dem."

"Which white men?" VD asked.

"Men like you," Batwa said. "Not men like them."

He nodded back down the track. They heard the sounds of soldiers coming after them. Saw torches flash in the trees and heard shouts.

"Can you lead us to the vehicles, Digger?" Hunt asked.

"Yeah, about a click up this track, maybe two, they drove us here from the ambush on the plane ride in," Digger said.

"Okay, Digger, you lead. Batwa, you help him. Fabrice, can you walk? We'll get those chains off you as soon as we can."

"Yes," Fabrice said quietly.

"Everybody else okay? VD, help with Lord Langdon. I'll guard the rear."

Digger handed him the rifle. Hunt checked the signal on the satellite phone.

Nothing.

CHAPTER THIRTY-TWO

It was early-dawn when they got to the edge of the dense forest. The sounds of the soldiers had fallen away. There was distance between them, but they knew that their tracks would be visible in the growing daylight and didn't have time. Digger and VD pulled the camouflage off the stashed Land Rovers and cleared the space. Maddy stood and shivered in her underwear.

"It's alright," Hunt said to her, "It's nearly over."

He checked the signal again. One bar.

"Please work," he said and dialled and lifted the phone to his year. It connected. An electronic voice said, "Please identify."

Hunt punched in an eight digit code.

"Enter codename."

"Boatman."

The others looked at him and waited. They looked unsure whether they were impressed or afraid.

"Connecting," the electronic voice said.

"Yes?" Hunt heard Soames' voice on a delay. It sounded digitised and distant, but it was him.

"Oh, thank God," Hunt said. "Gerry, it's Stirling."

Soames started to speak and the delayed signal cut him off. "You're alive. Thank God. What about Lord Langdon and the others?"

"Wait, Gerry, I don't have much time."

"Okay," Soames said. "Send, over."

"I need a transporter to the airfield in Côte d'Ambre. We have the hostages, alive. Scratcher requires urgent medical attention. Transport to be deployed now. Land Rover will rendezvous at airstrip in," he checked his watch, "approximately twelve-hours."

He paused. Soames came over the line difficult to hear but understandable.

"Roger," he said, "Transport will meet you there. Be advised. An Increment Squadron is inbound to your position. We were notified of your deaths. We thought you were dead. The Increment will be infiltrating with Chinook in approximately," there was a pause, "Fifteen hours —"

"Gerry," Hunt cut him off. "How did you hear of our deaths?"

The line went silent.

"Gerry?" Hunt said.

"The Director of Intelligence notified me."

Hunt was quiet for a moment. His mind raced.

"What about Gentry?" Soames asked.

"The target has been eliminated. I repeat," Hunt said, "McArthur Gentry is dead. If you trace the geo-location of this signal, the camp is approximately two clicks east of this position. But, they can't infiltrate by helicopter and the enemy are heavily armed and fortified. Call the attack off, Gerry do you hear? No need for more lives to be lost for that madman."

"I understand. Roger," Soames said.

"Gerry?" Hunt said.

"I am here."

"I need one more thing."

"Send, over."

"I need the jet standing by in London. I need to do something ... the mission isn't over."

"What?" Soames said, "What for?"

"Soames, can you do it?"

The line was silent again.

"Yes, I can get it. Hunt, what are you doing?"

"Gerry, just send an extraction team and transporter to the airstrip, and have the jet fuelled and waiting for me. Tell it to wait. Tell it to wait for me, *no matter what*. Confirm you understand?"

"I understand."

"Thanks Gerry. And try and get a message to du Toit. Earth-eye know how to get in touch. An army of Lord's Resistance soldiers are looking for blood. The Russians might be in danger."

HUNT HUNG UP THE PHONE. Maddy was cold and shaking. He went to one of the vehicles and pulled out an old blanket and wrapped her in it. He reached into his pocket and pulled out the stone he took from the pit. He put it in her cold, shaking hand. She looked down at it.

"I don't believe it," she said. "It's gold."

"Believe it," Hunt nodded and forced a smile. "You were right."

He hugged her tightly to warm her up. She put the gold back in his back pocket.

"You keep it," she said.

"What's the plan, Stirling?" Digger asked. He looked concerned.

"We need to get to the airstrip," Hunt said, "As soon as we can."

Digger gestured to Langdon lying on the back seat. Hunt went over and had a look.

"Okay, we need to get him medical treatment as soon as possible. He needs an I.V. and some medical attention."

"So, what do we do?" Maddy asked.

"These white men," Hunt said to Batwa, the pygmy, "Where are they?"

He pointed west.

"Roads? Vehicles?" Hunt asked.

The pygmy wobbled his head from side to side, "Dem roads carry 'dis. Can be get through."

"How far?"

The hunter put his hand to his chin and said, "Can be one hour, when road make 'dis not rain."

"The rain might have washed the roads out," Hunt said.

The pygmy nodded.

"Isn't that where du Toit and the Russians are?" Hunt asked Maddy.

She nodded. "Yes, I think so."

"That may be be our only option," Hunt said. "Load up the vehicles, find du Toit, and hope that they have medical supplies and an operating comms system. And we can warn them about the LRF ourselves."

"That's a good trade," VD said, trying to sound upbeat. "Priceless information that will save their lives in exchange for some medical supplies and a free phone call."

"Okay," Hunt said. "Batwa, you sit in front, with me. Digger, you drive. Maddy, look after Langdon as best you can. Fabrice, you help Digger. VD —"

He was already clambering into the front of the lead Land Rover. He leaned out of the open door and said, "Quit your chin wagging. Let's get out of here. No time to waste."

Hunt gave a grin and winked at Maddy.

"Let's go."

VD AND HUNT were in one Land Rover heading west. Hunt could see the other Land Rover as it swayed and jolted behind. Batwa sat in the back and leaned between them.

VD turned to Hunt and said, "So, what's the plan?"

"What do you mean?"

"What's with the need for the Vail jet?"

Hunt shook his head. He was concentrating on the narrow trail that was supposed to be a road. It was made of red slippery earth. Water had washed big channels into it and the Land Rover swayed ominously from side to side as if it might roll. It was a slow speed, but better than movement on foot. They were contouring around a block of primary jungle. The steep verge of a grassed hill on one side and the thick trucks of indigenous trees on the other.

Batwa pointed, "White men this way," he said.

"Better hope it's the Russians," VD said.

Hunt heard a low grumble, the deep start of a lion's roar. The sound rolled through them like thunder.

"What the hell is that?"

"Oh, my God, look —" VD said and pointed at Mount Lamia. A thin plume of white ash shot straight up out of it.

"Great Mama very angry," Batwa said, and then everything was moving. Hunt and VD were knocked from side to side. The trees outside shook and swayed. Hunt pulled the hand-brake and tried to stop the vehicle from sliding down the slope. It happened fast and violently. Trees crashed and fell into one another. Birds took flight. The energy created a storm of electrons around them. Hunt held onto the door as the Land Rover slid. They were almost on their side and he saw something he'd only heard about. An explosive flash of lightning that travelled from the top of Mount Lamia into the clouds. Batwa covered his eyes and chanted a prayer. All around trees were cracking and splitting. The Land Rover was slipping down the slope.

"Quick!" Hunt shouted over the rolling thunder. "Get out! Follow me."

He forced the door open and pulled Batwa out of the back. The brave pygmy stood and held onto Hunt's hand. The ground beneath the Land Rover gave way. Hunt grabbed onto VD and held Batwa's hand. They piled out of the vehicle as it went sideways down the slope with a mudslide. What felt like minutes, was over in seconds. Hunt just lay face down trying to work it all out.

The Land Rover behind them missed the shifting earth. Maddy jumped out.

"Are you okay?" she yelled over to them.

Hunt got up and sat with his knees under his chin. He started to laugh. VD joined him, and then Batwa. They laughed hysterically. Deep, booming, raucous laughter.

Hunt waved to Maddy. They were alright. The Land Rover was on its side, halfway down the slope. It wouldn't get out of there.

"Looks like we're walking again," Hunt said.

"How far, Batwa?" VD asked.

"No far, jus through da trees," he said and pointed again.

VD shook his head, "T.I.A."

"This is Africa," Hunt said.

"T.I.A." Batwa agreed.

CHAPTER THIRTY-THREE

Fabrice carried Langdon through the primary jungle like a bride over the threshold. Hunt walked ahead with Batwa. They were following a muddy man-made path through the forest. Batwa stopped.

"White men 'der," he said and pointed. He was afraid.

Hunt looked, but couldn't see anything. He looked back, but Batwa was moving back from him. The pygmies had survived for centuries as shadows in the vast jungle. Hunt let him go, and moved around a corner in the path. A man with a giant bald head, was standing there. He was in dark sunglasses, camouflage gear, and with one hand resting on a black submachine gun. The tremors kept up. The official looking sign, written in Cyrillic script, was shaking. Hunt heard activity ahead. Lots of movement and engines revving. He put his hands up and stepped out into the path so the Russian could see him.

"Halt!" the guard commanded and lifted his rifle.

"We're the British expedition," Hunt said. "We're in trouble and have a sick man here. We know Servaas du Toit, Colonel du Toit, do you know him?"

The guard lowered his weapon and spoke into a shoulder mounted mic.

"You're just in time," the guard said in a heavy Russian accent. "Evacuation in progress."

"Come on!" Hunt called out to the group. "Hurry, hurry. No time."

Fabrice walked past Hunt with sweat running down his face. He was straining. As VD passed he said, "He won't let anyone help him."

They made their way past the guard and he nodded.

"Just keep down this path," he said. "Compound beyond tree line."

Hunt waited for the group to pass by. They looked like refugees fleeing a war. They were tired, dirty and ragged. Hunt heard the revving engine fighting through the mud and slush and saw an open top Jeep approaching.

du Toit was hanging out the side and the Jeep pulled up with a skid to the group of stragglers. du Toit yelled to the perimeter guard, "Ivan! Come on," and called him over with his hand. du Toit studied the group and shook his head.

"Jesus Christ. Did you feel that? The ground was shaking. Our sensors and equipment went crazy. You're ones for good timing, huh? We're just checking out of this Hotel California nightmare," he said. He saw Fabrice straining with Langdon and said, "What the hell do we have here."

"Prime Minister's son," Hunt said.

He climbed out and cleared space in the back of the Jeep.

"He's in a state. Come on, put him in here," du Toit said and Fabrice lifted Langdon gently into the back seat. "We're leaving," du Toit said to no-one in particular. "Climb in Ivan. We need to get this man to the med centre."

The big Russian looked at the back seat and shook his head, "I walk." And he set off for the compound.

"How're you getting out?" Hunt asked.

"Boats by the river," he said. "Packing them with gear and

getting out of here. If you want to catch it, you'd better move your sorry arses."

"Where are you headed?" Hunt said.

"Christ man, do you really care? We are getting the hell out of here. Come on, Maddy get in here. Take her back to camp," du Toit said.

The old Colonel joined the team on the walk back to the compound. It was only a hundred meters, but it opened up like a construction site. du Toit pointed to a collapsed tree. It had fallen on top of a series of containers.

"Our old headquarters, nearly killed one of our guys," du Toit said. "They reckon that mountain top is going to blow. We need to get out of here."

Hunt and du Toit went over to another container. A sign read SibPlat Med Centre, and had the same in Cyrillic. The name of the Russian mining company. Lord Langdon was in there getting treatment, along with another man from the company. du Toit spoke to the doctor and the nurse. His hands moved like they always did and it sounded like he was imploring them to move faster. Hunt stepped outside and took a deep breath of the morning air. He saw a Russian Mil Mi-8 transport helicopter sitting on a makeshift landing pad. du Toit stepped out.

"Crazy Russians," he said and shook his head.

"What about that?" Hunt asked and pointed to the chopper.

"What about it?"

"Why aren't you evacuating in the helo?"

du Toit pointed his thumb over his shoulder, "Because, the man who can fly it is in the bed next to Lord Langdon. He was in the headquarters when the tree collapsed."

Hunt thought for a moment. He knew Digger could fly.

"How much do you want for her?" Hunt asked.

"What do you mean? You want to buy it?"

"Or lease ... we could medevac your pilot."

du Toit shook his head. He was unsure and watched the activity around him. Men and women rushing back and forth, packing Jeeps and trucks.

"Do you know we cut a road through this jungle to the river?" du Toit said absentmindedly.

"How much?" Hunt asked, and broke into du Toit's thoughts.

"You can't afford it," he said. "Forget it. You can come out with us."

"We have a jet waiting at Kissidou Airstrip in Amber Coast."

"So?" du Toit said.

"Give us the chopper and we'll evacuate your man," Hunt said and nodded toward the helicopter.

"No chance, Hunt. I can't spare the aircraft."

But Hunt could see that du Toit was thinking. "Christ," VD came over and pitched in, "You have a helicopter just sitting there and no pilot? We have a pilot. Help us out."

"Name your price," Hunt said.

"Five-hundred thousand."

"I'll do you one better," Hunt pulled out the gold stone and tossed it to du Toit. The throw surprised him, but he juggled it in his palms and held on to it.

"The hell is this?" he said as he inspected it. Hunt saw the yellow light shine off his skin. "My God. Where did you get this?"

"Give us the chopper and I'll give you the coordinates. You'll get your half a percent of return from all primary deposits," Hunt said. du Toit kept on looking at the stone and back up at Hunt and back to the stone.

"Tell me where it is," du Toit said.

"The reef is as tall as my arm. And who knows how long. Give us the chopper and you will get your gold."

It was an offer too good to turn down.

du Toit put out his hand and they shook. They had a deal.

"I am going to need that back though," Hunt said, and put his hand out for the stone. "And," he added, "I need one more thing ..."

du Toit gave him a curious look that turned to a knowing grin. He realised Hunt had saved the best for last. "Cheeky bugger," the old Colonel laughed. "What is it?"

"I need you to do something. I need you to get me an audience with Mabosongo. Can you do it?"

du Toit glanced at VD and they both looked at Hunt.

"The President?" VD asked.

"Can you do it?" Hunt asked.

THE ROTORS of the Mil Mi-8 transport helicopter turned at an idle.

The high-pitched whine of the engines spun the long blades faster and faster. Digger checked his instrumentation. VD was in the front with him.

Hunt looked out from the back of the military transport chopper. The Russians had done a demolition job on the jungle. They blasted sites for buildings and containers. There were mechanical diggers and equipment scattered around a large parcel of land. The helicopter's blades spun in the middle of a clearing blasted for resupply and extraction. Hunt saw two security guys carrying Lord Langdon to the helicopter on a stretcher. He was covered in a blanket and the nurses held an IV drip. They ducked low under the wash in a hurry and slid the stretcher into the helicopter. They slammed the sliding door.

The rotors spun at a blur. du Toit stood with his hands on his hip and waved. He pointed to his watch and mouthed, 'bring her back.' He'd said he would come and collect the loaned helicopter from the airstrip.

"Thank God for greed," Hunt said. Maddy sat next to him and studied the stone laced with gold.

"What?" she asked and looked up.

"Nothing."

She looked at him quizzically.

"Just glad you're safe."

CHAPTER THIRTY-FOUR

ZERMATT, SWITZERLAND

Sir William Alexander-Young sat outside in the sunshine. The air was crisp and cool. He loved Zermatt in the summer. Fewer tourists and plenty of challenging hikes. He was in the steep sloped valley, looking up at the Matterhorn, and enjoying a glass of Champagne after a strong walk around the base of the horned mountain.

The restaurant, Royaume du Cervin, was full. People sat out in the sun and spoke French and German and children ran in-between them and played on the green-yellow grass. It was an idyllic scene. Just what he needed after the last few weeks in London. The Clubhouse had become tense and pressured. His wife was deciding whether to have the pecan pie with cream or ice-cream when he heard the sound of the rotors. The noise was distant at first. Some of the tables stopped talking and glanced up. They were used to rescue helicopters in the winter, but less so in the warm, dry, summer months.

Sir William shielded his eyes from the sun and glanced up as the red and white Air Zermatt helicopter flashed overhead. It did a big loop and turned and came down softly on a grass clearing to the side of the restaurant. The onlookers protected their faces from the wash. Sir William wiped a napkin across his mouth and watched as the sliding door of the helicopter's side door slid open and a black clad man in wraparound sunglasses stepped out. He was the size of a heavyweight. Tall and lean, in fighting shape.

"Operative," Sir William said to himself with his mouth full.

"What?" his wife asked.

"Never mind."

He threw down his napkin as the man clad in black approached.

"Sir William?" the man said and stood in front of the table.

Sir William nodded, "Yes."

"Could you come with me, Sir, I have an important message."

All of the surrounding tables looked.

"Well, let's hear it."

"Sir, I really think it better I brief you in private. I have the information," he gestured and looked back, "in the chopper."

"Alright, then. Let's get this over with. Honey," he said as he stood, "I'll be back. Order me a pecan pie with ice-cream."

"Yes, dear."

HUNT WALKED SLIGHTLY behind Sir William. As they approached the helicopter he had a single glance back at the restaurant. The people were sipping on beer in the sun and laughing and paying no more attention.

"Right, who are you?" Sir William shouted over the idling rotors. "And what do you want?"

Hunt put his arm out to guide the Director of Intelligence closer to the door.

"Please get in, Sir. I have the information you need."

Sir William looked reproachful. He glanced back at the restaurant and his wife. Hunt moved across and subtly cut him off and beckoned him to climb in.

"What the hell is all this about? It'd better be good. My ice-cream is melting."

Sir William climbed into the chopper and Hunt followed him. Hunt sat opposite and gave Digger the thumbs up in the front seat.

"Right, what is it?"

Hunt leaned forward and slammed the sliding door shut. The helicopter lifted off.

"What the hell are you doing!? Let me out this instant." Sir William lunged for the door, but Hunt put his foot across in front of him.

"Sit back, relax. It'll all be over in a minute."

"Wait. I know you ... Don't I know you?"

Hunt crossed his arms and put his head back.

"You're that operative of Gerry's, what's your codename ..." Sir William clicked his fingers and tried to recall. "Boatman, isn't it?"

Hunt said nothing.

THE HELICOPTER FLEW fifty miles to Sion International Airport and landed a short walk away from the private jet. Hunt opened the sliding door.

"Get out," he said.

"What? Where are you taking me? What do you think you're doing? This is treason!"

"Oh, yeah? Well, that makes two of us then. Climb out. Get in the jet. Don't say another word."

Digger was looking back at them from the front seat. He shook the pilot's hand and slipped him a thick envelope. The Air Zermatt pilot grinned and gave a mock salute.

"You'll never get away with this," Sir William said as he climbed out and looked up at Hunt.

"Maybe not," Hunt said with disdain, "But then again, neither will you."

VD waited onboard for them and greeted the Director of Intelligence with a knowing grin.

"Who the hell are you?" Sir William said.

"Welcome aboard, Sir," VD said. "Please take your seat. Make sure overhead lockers are stowed and your seat belt is tightly fastened. If you cause any fuss you'll be bound and gagged like the criminal you are."

Sir William opened his mouth to protest, but VD just indicated a seat in the rear of the plush private jet and he went and sat down. He was talking to himself and remonstrating silently. Hunt boarded the aircraft and Sir William immediately shouted from the back, "I'll have your head for this!"

VD shook his head and walked over to him.

"I did warn you," he said, and Sir William spent the take off strapped to his chair.

They hit cruising altitude and the pilot's voice came over the intercom. "Folks, we're at forty-one thousand feet, flight time to Puerto-Nuevo is approximately six-and-a-half hours. Settle in. Relax. We'll take care of you."

William Alexander-Young's eyes widened and he struggled in his seat. His muffled cries carried on, like a puppy whining, in the back of the plane.

VD, Digger and Hunt settled in and ignored him.

CHAPTER THIRTY-FIVE

REPUBLIC OF EQUATORIAL VARRISSA, WEST AFRICA

Hunt had vivid and terrible dreams. He slept restlessly. He was standing at the graves of his parents. He was in his suit in the rain. Water seeped through. He heard voices. Something from beyond the grave. It called out to him. He twisted in his seat. The boy in the dream called out to his mother, but she was gone. Hunt jolted awake. He listened to the quiet hum and drone of the airplane cabin. It was cold. He saw the sun coming up purple and deep blue over the horizon. Digger was awake. He stopped cleaning the automatic rifle in his hands and looked at Hunt.

"Bad dreams?" Digger asked.

"Just the Taliban coming out of the cupboards again ..." Hunt replied.

Digger nodded. Hunt knew he knew. The faces of the dead never left. They flashed in his mind like a cascade of playing cards.

"I like to clean my weapons when that happens," he said with a sympathetic smile and paused. "What do you think will happen?" Digger asked.

Hunt looked out the window and shook his head. Sir William was in the back, restrained and in a different state of restlessness.

"Don't know, but it can all go wrong very fast," he said.

Digger was quiet.

"We just have to trust du Toit, and use our guile," Hunt said.

"No back-up plan ..." Digger said contemplatively and wiped the barrel of the assault rifle.

Hunt knew what he meant. Two is one and one is none. Two plans mean you have one. One plan means you have none, if it goes wrong. It was a bad position, in a very high-stakes game of poker. Hunt was all in. He'd shown his hand, and now he waited for the other players to play into him. If du Toit had been successful in arranging, or at least, preparing the ground for an audience with President Mabosongo, it was all to play for. If not, well, it was all over. A busted flush.

The pilot came over the intercom. They wouldn't have long to find out what cards the other players had. VD stirred. Hunt looked back and Alexander-Young's eyes were open wide and afraid. Probably how the betrayed ex-Special Forces soldiers being held in Black Beach felt, Hunt thought.

THE JET JUDDERED and shook as it descended into the hotbed of cruelty and dissent. It hit the deck with a skid and rattled along the runway. Hunt tucked a Browning 9mm pistol into his belt and adjusted his kevlar vest. VD and Digger checked and rechecked their Galil ACE 31's. Big weapons with big stopping power. What they lacked in numbers, the three old Special Forces veterans, would make up for with firepower and surprise. VD patted his grenades and Digger checked his pistol. They were ready for whatever was going to be on the other side of the aircraft doors when they opened onto the tarmac in Equatorial Varrissa. Hunt felt the tension in his spine. The cabin was cool, but he was sweating. Being back in this godforsaken place made the bite on his arm ache. He closed his eyes and took a breath. It was go time.

The jet came to a stop. The three men stood at the exit, ready for anything. Sir William looked anxious and afraid. Digger and VD held their rifles like they were about to burst through the passenger exit door. Hunt nodded to them and they nodded back. He pulled the handles and the door popped and swung open. VD and Digger each went one way and cleared their arcs out onto the runway. It was quiet.

"I don't see anything."

VD leaned back in and shook his head. Hunt sighed. This wasn't good. He felt the morning heat settle around the aircraft. Sweat dripped off him now. There was a heat shimmer out on the tarmac already. Hunt saw something in the haze. Two vehicles approached. They moved at speed. Hunt saw armed men standing up with rifles.

"We've got incoming," Digger said.

"Here we go boys, let's stay frosty. No matter what," Hunt said. "You got it?"

VD nodded, "Welcome party is running a little late."

"Sit tight and don't make any noise!" Hunt said and pointed at Sir William.

A screech of tyres and shouting came from outside. VD and Digger were in a kneeling position with their rifles covering the arcs. Uniformed soldiers jumped from the Jeeps and scattered. They aimed their weapons back at the cabin. Just then the pilot came out.

"What the hell is going on?" he asked. He was panicked and uncertain.

"Go back to the controls," Hunt ordered and pointed. "Stay there. If we say so, get this thing airborne, no matter what. Understand?"

He nodded briskly and hurried back into the cockpit. Hunt looked out. A tall man in a loose fitting beret strode forward. He put his hand on his hip and looked up at them.

"Hello? Who am I talking with, please?" he said.

"A bit polite for this time of the morning," Digger said out the corner of his mouth.

VD gave a snort of approval.

"What do we tell them?" Digger asked.

"Let's just wait. See what they say," Hunt said.

The man on the tarmac broke out in a wide smile. "Good morning gentlemen. I am afraid the President is unavoidably detained at the moment," he said, "I am Brigadier Fitzgerald. You can talk to me. I am told you have something for us."

VD looked at Digger and mouthed, 'Fitzgerald' and gave Digger a quizzical look.

"I need to speak to the President," Hunt said.

"And, who might you be?" the Brigadier asked.

"I'd really prefer to discuss this with Mabosongo. We agreed on a swap ..."

"Yes," the Brigadier said, "du Toit was found to be unclear. What is it exactly that you have to trade with us?"

"I don't see any of the prisoners here, Brigadier, this was supposed to be a straight swap. A trade of prisoners. You have seventeen mercenaries in Black Beach. We want to swap for them."

The Brigadier let out a throaty laugh and paused.

"Mister ..."

"Hunt."

"Mister Hunt, I do not know of these mercenaries you speak of, but if they are in Black Beach, they are criminals. And, if they are criminals, they are most likely dead. You see, we do not tolerate disobedience here in the Republic. And, furthermore, you've landed illegally in the Republic and are talking of a trade, but we have no idea what it is you want to trade us *with*."

He took off his beret and dabbed the sweat from his forehead and glanced at his men with their rifles aimed at the door of the aircraft.

"Now, it is very hot, Mister Hunt. I am likely to go insane in this heat. I need to go in, where it is cool. Come out of the plane. Put your weapons down."

Hunt shook his head.

"That isn't going to happen, Brigadier."

"Come, come. There is no way out. You are surrounded. Let us stop these silly, silly games. I think you must be smarter than that. Put down your weapons or we will kill you all."

"You can try," Hunt said, "but your men will also die."

Hunt saw some of the soldiers glance at one another and said, "We are prepared to die here on this runway. Are you?"

The Brigadier rubbed his chin.

"What is this thing you have to trade for the lives of the criminals?"

"I have the location of the traitor McArthur Gentry and his guerrillas."

"We already know where Gentry is," the Brigadier said.

He was emphatic. Hunt called his bluff.

"If you knew, you would have found him already."

"We have reports that say Gentry is dead. There was a mutiny and he was sacrificed."

Hunt shook his head, "I was there. I saw McArthur Gentry. He is alive." He paused. "Anyway, wouldn't you want confirmation and to destroy his forces? I am sure the President would like to parade the corpse like a prize through the city, maybe as a warning. What do you say?"

The Brigadier signalled to one of the soldiers and he went to the Jeep and spoke into a handheld radio.

He came back and spoke to the Brigadier.

"Okay. Put your weapons down and come with us. Put them down or we will kill you!" the Brigadier demanded.

Hunt shook his head again. "No. We won't put them down and we won't come with you. Do you hear that sound?" Hunt tilted his ear skyward and pointed. The Brigadier looked up.

"You might not be able to see it, but it can see you. If you kill us, the UK Special Forces will rain missiles down on you like a bolt of lightning. Unarmed aerial vehicle. Your President will not survive."

The Brigadier was silent. He glanced at the sky. He was unsure.

"So," the Brigadier said. "What now?"

Hunt thought for a moment.

"I will come with you. But, you need to leave a man as collateral," Hunt said.

VD shook his head, "No, don't do it. They'll torture you."

"It's okay, I'm counting on it," Hunt said quietly, then, "Well, Brigadier, are you interested?"

"What if du Toit sold you out? Like he did to Maddy with the Russians?"

"A risk I'll have to take," Hunt said.

CHAPTER THIRTY-SIX

Hunt gave his sidearm to VD and put his hands up. He stepped off the jet. Digger followed him down and took hold of the soldier. The soldier didn't look impressed that the Brigadier left him as collateral. Hunt knew it was more symbolic than an insurance policy. Hunt was immediately grabbed by the soldiers and pulled into a Jeep. He didn't resist.

"We'll wait," Digger said. "But, don't be too long."

He sat in the back and they raced through town. The airport was on the western extremity. Roadblocks and guard posts with armed soldiers opened barriers for the convoy of Jeeps as they sped through the potholed and crumbling streets. All around women carried containers of water on their heads and stray dogs sniffed and scratched through rubbish that lined the road. Hunt could see the white gleaming concave tower of the presidential palace rising up in front.

The harbour and port section of Puerto-Nuevo was a walled off complex on a peninsula that included the opulent palace, military barracks, Black Beach Prison and suburban residential homes in the colonial fashion, inhabited by the people President Mabosongo wanted closest to him. They drove up to an eight foot high green steel gate. The guard gave the signal and two other soldiers heaved and pushed the barrier open. Inside it looked like another world. The Jeep jolted forward and they drove over the bridge running over a section of the Rio Moa that created a natural barrier between the fortress and the rest of the country. Hunt could see the stately and well maintained roads, telephone poles and guard towers interspersed amongst the palm trees. Mabosongo had holed himself up in a fortress.

Intelligence reports suggested Mabosongo was paranoid and hardly ever left the port compound and relative safety of the palace. Over decades, mostly spent murdering his own people, he'd developed a paranoia bordering on psychosis. He feared assassination and suspected plots to topple his power from all corners of his government. His people lived in as much fear of him as he did of them. Every time the President had a bad dream there were arrests and public executions. Rumour said he personally supervised the torture sessions. Unconfirmed, as there were never any survivors to talk about it. He'd never left the country. When he ventured from the port compound it was only surrounded by a heavily armed and fearless presidential guard who were sworn to protect him, and who were treated like demigods. Weapons, whiskey and wives.

The Jeep pulled up to another high wall laced with razor wire and pieces of broken glass. It was once a cream-white colour, but was now stained with black sludge and brown rust. A square concrete building ran right up to the wall. It almost overhung it. The windows were lined with steel bars and wire. He was looking at Black Beach Prison.

They drove through the clanking steel gate. There was a sombre mood in the concrete lot. A shadow was cast by the prison building. The stench of human shit. It was suddenly cold. Hunt felt like a bull being led into a slaughterhouse. He wanted to run, but he was locked into a one way conveyor marching to his own death. And he knew it.

The soldier next to him in the back turned his head. Hunt locked eyes with the cold, misty-eyed stare. There was a moment of hesitation and the soldier lunged. He put a black canvas bag over Hunt's head. There was a tussle, until Hunt heard a pistol cock, and the hard metal pressed against his head. His captors never spoke. Just handled him roughly and pushed him in the direction they wanted him to go. His head was bowed under the hood. It was hard to breathe. He stumbled and they let him fall to one knee before lifting him again. He could feel the cold chill of the tiled floors and the echoey hollowness and deep darkness of the concrete passages. The sound of fluorescent light bulbs flickering and water dripping overwhelmed his senses and they recoiled. Fight or flight took over. He had nowhere run, and it was a fight he couldn't win. Unless death was victory. Stay frosty.

He heard the clank and slam of a bolt unlatched. He felt the cool air as the door opened. They pushed him in and down into a metal chair and pulled the hood off. Hunt sat at a rectangular steel table with his head bowed. It was a small white-tiled room. Cold and echoey, like a butcher's walk-in fridge. A wide metallic reflective glass looked back at him. The room was long and dark. Half of it was in shadow. A single bare bulb hung down over his head and water dripped from it and onto the steel table. They came back and hand-cuffed him to the chair. He kept thinking of the soldiers who were in here. The reason he had come back. What they were subjected to. Their lives traded for oil and gold. Sacrifices at the altar of power and greed.

He heard a rustle in the dark end of the room. He wasn't alone. There was the flick of the match and the sulphur and potassium chlorate ignited and the flame cast a shadow on a round and pockmarked face. The smell of tobacco hit his nose and the figure dragged long and deep on a stubby cigarillo.

"Smoking is a terrible habit, don't you think Agent Hunt? It bends men to its will like nothing else. Here, it is currency. Men kill for cigarettes. Debts are paid with them," the voice in the darkness said. The only thing Hunt could see was the glow of the thin cigar. "Imagine, a human life worth less than a cigarette. There is something beautiful in the simplicity." Water dripped and lights buzzed. "Would you care for one? I received them as a gift from Castro. He is quite generous ... for a communist."

Hunt said nothing. The silence closed in on the cell like an ice on the wind.

"No, thank you, Excellency," Hunt said.

The shadow snorted at the title. Hunt could tell he was smiling.

"I am curious. Why did you decide to give yourself up to my men? Aren't you afraid?"

Hunt shivered involuntarily in the gloomy cold.

"Because I knew you would be here," he said. "You attend all of the torture sessions."

"*Supervise*. I believe my file says, supervise. Still, it was a gamble. How do you know you wouldn't simply be shot, like the low life assassin you are?"

Hunt paused. He tried to remain calm under the glare and the duress. The shadow exhaled a thick cloud of cigar smoke and gave a little cough and cleared his throat.

"I think you're an intelligent man, President Mabosongo. I think you'd want to hear what I have to tell you ..."

"About Gentry?" he asked. It was dismissive and he gave another snort.

"About Gentry. Something else too."

"Enlighten me."

"I have information."

There was the scrape of metal on tile. The shadow stood.

He clicked his fingers and the overhead spotlights buzzed and clanked to life. The room was immediately bright. Hunt closed his eyes against the flash. When he opened them a figure in brown military number two dress with a Sam Browne belt and row of medals approached the table. Hunt could see streaks and splashes of dried blood on the walls and floor. The President's shoes squelched on the sticky floor as he walked up to the steel table and put his hand on it. Hunt could smell his tobacco breath, and as if he were a wild animal, tried to avoid direct eye contact.

"You cannot even look at me ..." Mabosongo said. His voice was laced with spite and pity. "Tell me what you have to tell me, and while you do, I will decide what to do with you and your precious coup plotters."

Hunt could sense the rage building in this man's chest. He could hear his own heart, beating like a bass drum, and the swoosh of blood inside his head.

It was real fear. Tiny pupils. Lump in your throat. Want to scream. Fear.

"I know who was behind the coup attempt," Hunt said and tried to mask the jitter.

Mabosongo stood and straightened his jacket. He checked his watch.

"I don't have time for this. Start talking." He turned and paced in front of the table while Hunt spoke.

"You rejected the British concession."

"Some time ago," the President agreed.

"In favour of the Russians or the Chinese. Possibly as a negotiating tactic? Well, certain interests wanted to ensure that that didn't happen. They also wanted to ensure control of the concessions for the foreseeable future."

"It is simply economic, rather than political colonialism, Agent Hunt."

Hunt shrugged. The reasons weren't important. Only that he realised the men he had in prison were worthless to him.

"You're not telling me anything I don't already know," the President said. "And time is the only thing I cannot give you."

"The whole coup was a setup," Hunt said. "Gentry, Lord Langdon, the militia. It was a conspiracy to start a war and reimpose a managed transition to a government friendly to UK business interests."

This caught Mabosongo's attention. He walked back over to the desk opposite Hunt and pulled out his green leather chair. It was something to see him sitting on elegant lounge furniture in the middle of a human-blood splattered cell. He lit another cigarillo and leaned back.

"Continue," he said with the wave of a hand.

"Gentry was a set up to disrupt the coup. Lord Langdon was set up. Someone wanted to use Langdon's power and connections to focus attention on Equatorial Varrissa. They tipped Gentry off, ensuring that he kidnapped Langdon. You were to be blamed. The rescue, our rescue mission, was never supposed to succeed. We were going to be front page news in a public relations campaign to get the Prime Minister to invade and topple your government. The headlines would read, 'Prime Minister's son murdered in African jungle' and 'President refused foreign troops to intervene.'"

Mabosongo narrowed his eyes and tapped the ash. He lifted his leg and dropped it on the desk.

"Continue ..."

"Well, aren't you interested in who set you up?" Hunt asked.

"Why should I be? I have seventeen coup plotters behind bars. I have a spy sent by MI6. I have your confession. What else do I need?"

"The British government doesn't care about me. They don't care about the men you have in prison. Lord Langdon is back, safe and sound, sitting at home drinking tea and listening to the BBC World Service."

"I don't need to explain myself to you," Mabosongo said.

"Unless your government claims you in twenty-four hours, you will be tried as a common criminal and hung from the gates of the prison as a warning."

"What if I told you who was behind the coup?"

The President took his foot off the desk and twisted to sit face on. The white smoke and thick smell of tobacco and blood hung heavy in the air.

"It makes no difference to me," Mabosongo said. "You're a foreign spy. You can't be trusted."

Mabosongo eyed him up. "You are captive. You have no plan. No backup. No hope of escape. Men like you would say anything to get free."

Hunt wondered if he was coming across as desperate. He doubted it.

"I came willingly, Excellency." Hunt let the words hang, then added, "What if I knew the location of a reef of gold thicker than my arm ... If I said I could give you Gentry's location, the seam of gold, and the person responsible for the plot to overthrow you?"

Hunt had his attention.

"What do I give you for all of this information?"

"The hostages. They are worthless to you. And safe passage for myself and my friends, out of the Republic," Hunt said. "That is all."

He nodded and thought. "And so, who was it, behind this conspiracy?" President Mabosongo said. His tone was measured. He seemed calm, but Hunt sensed an undercurrent of tension. A single bead of sweat ran down the President's forehead. He wiped it away with a flick of his fingers.

"A Director of Intelligence at the Secret Intelligence Service," Hunt said. "A senior person in the UK Government, and also a traitor to his country. Corrupt, with no redeeming qualities."

"And where is this man?"

"First tell me, do we have a deal?"

"If what you say is true. I would consider this."

"You get a high ranking official from the UK. You have the evidence of treason and conspiracy. You would have leverage for the Republic on an international level. You could even renegotiate the terms of the concession, if you knew where the gold was ..."

CHAPTER THIRTY-SEVEN

Hunt sat at the steel table and waited. The psychotic President of Equatorial Varrissa mulled the offer in his head. Hunt knew this man was not driven by the normal motivations and desires of human beings. He had some God-like complex that required the total and continuous show of force. A demonstration of power that could stretch as far as it could.

Mabosongo stood. He took a long drag on the thin cigarillo and looked at the tip as it burned. He walked over and sat down on the edge of his desk.

"You'd better not be lying to me, foreign spy," the President said. "Who is the Director of Intelligence you have to trade?"

"Sir William Alexander-Young."

Hunt saw a glint in the President's eye. He knew the name. He might even know the man personally.

"And where is this man?"

"He's in Varrissa," Hunt said.

The President studied him. His face was a picture of dubiousness.

"Do we have a deal?" Hunt asked and swallowed.

The President leaned in and Hunt leaned his head back.

He strained against the restraints. The President's pock-marked face and brown teeth were close to his face. Mabosongo reached out and wiped the palm of his hand on Hunt's face and sniffed his hand. He shook his head.

"You people stink," he said.

Hunt stayed leaning back. He dared not breathe or look this man in the eye. He treated him like a rabid dog, no eye contact. Slow movements. Mabosongo lifted the cigarillo and pushed it slowly towards Hunt's eye.

"Are you lying to me?"

Hunt shook his head. He felt the burning ends of tightly bundled tobacco.

"You see a lot," the President said. "Maybe we should find out how well you see with only one eye. Hmm?"

Hunt was sweating. Stay frosty, stay frosty, he said to himself over and over. Don't react. The President stood abruptly. He walked to the heavy steel door and Hunt heard the bolt unlatch. The door swung open and cool, musty air flowed into the room. Hunt heard the tortured screams of other prisoners in other cells. The slap of metal on flesh. The sounds of hopelessness. The President of Equatorial Varrissa turned to face him.

"Very well, Agent Hunt. I will accept your offer," Mabosongo said. He gestured to Brigadier Fitzgerald. "Speak to this man about the prisoner swap. I want detailed coordinates of the site and the mine. When the Brigadier is content, you can leave. We will then conduct the swap. Those are my terms."

Hunt nodded. He had no other choice. His life and those of his friends were in the hands of a known collector of human skulls. The Brigadier stepped inside the cell. The President held Hunt's gaze for a moment and turned. His polished brown shoes clacked away down the corridor.

HUNT SAT in the front passenger seat of a Jeep and saw the jet's stairs lowering as he approached. He was still hand-cuffed. Behind him was a convoy of military four-tonne trucks. Their diesel engines whined and groaned and the trucks shuddered and pulled their way along.

All seventeen prisoners were in the back, along with about the same number of heavily armed presidential guards. Hunt had only caught a glimpse of the prisoners being loaded. They looked thin, beaten, and covered in filth. His mind raced. He hoped Digger and VD wouldn't open fire on them. Hunt saw Digger leaning out of the open door. He guessed VD would be with Sir William, preparing him for the handover.

The Equatorial Varrissans wanted to make a show of it. There were to be television cameras and photographers. This was an international public relations opportunity for Debby the dictator and he wasn't going to miss it. The Jeep and the four-tonne trucks pulled up alongside the jet. Hunt gave a nod and Digger waved. The driver leaned over and uncuffed Hunt's wrists. He rubbed them.

"I am going to speak to my men," Hunt said, and the soldier shrugged.

He climbed out of the Jeep. The drivers of the trucks waited. The sun pressed down on them. Hunt squinted against the glare. Soldiers climbed down and stood around cradling their weapons. The airport was eerie and quiet.

Hunt went to the bottom of the stairs. He stood with his hands on his hips and spoke to Digger without looking at him.

"Make sure Alexander-Young is untied. He needs to look natural, not like he is a prisoner," Hunt said, and Digger relayed the message inside the aircraft to VD.

"Tell the pilot to get ready to go," Hunt said, and again Digger yelled the message inside.

Once he'd delivered the message, Digger leaned out again.

"What's the plan, Stirling?" he asked.

Hunt gave a little shake of his head.

"I don't know. We are waiting for the press. They want to make a big song and dance. We'll get the boys off those trucks and onto the aircraft and soon as they are loaded, we are out of here."

The pilot had gone through his start procedure and Hunt heard the second engine start spinning. The soldiers became active, like lizards after lying in the sun. They moved around the trucks and started waving their hands and speaking aggressively. Hunt ignored them initially. One came up and pointed his weapon at him. Hunt batted it away and stared him down.

"Get out of my face," he said. The soldier eyed him up. One of his colleagues said something in their native dialect and the aggressive one thought better of it. He spat on the ground in front of Hunt. The first engine turned over and started spinning. Hunt checked his watch. "Come on, come on."

A camera man and a reporter in a skirt were running across the tarmac towards them. The Brigadier sprung to life. He wandered over to the camera and the soldiers made a show of trying to stop them from coming any closer. Digger threw out a cap and sunglasses to Hunt and he put them on. He wrapped a shemagh around his neck and mouth. The last thing he needed was to be identified on television. The Brigadier gave an interview with lots of arm movements and belly laughs. Hunt thought of the prisoners sitting underneath the heavy olive canvas in the back of the trucks.

"Screw it," Hunt said and moved around to the back of the trucks. At first the soldiers didn't notice. They were posing and trying to get on the evening news. One glanced up as Hunt walked around the back. He shouted, "Hey! Stop!" Hunt didn't listen. The soldier ran up and lifted his rifle. He held it in front of Hunt's face. The cameraman heard the commotion and left the Brigadier standing there. He ran over with the camera and pointed it at Hunt and the soldier. They stood, death stare to death stare. Hunt was passive, but he had a crazed look in his eye. The soldier had beads of sweat running down his face and into his eyes. He sniffed.

"Go on then, do it," Hunt said, softly at first, then rising with his rage. "Do it! Do it!" He grabbed the muzzle and jabbed it into his chest. "Do it!"

The soldier looked panicked. The Brigadier rushed over and pushed the soldier away and stepped in front of the camera's lens. He put on a brave smile and tried to laugh it off.

"Come on, let's get this over with, before one of these men dies inside here," Hunt said to him. The Brigadier looked at Hunt and he raised his eyebrows.

"Yes, well, as you can see, we will now get this show on the road, excuse me," the Brigadier said to the camera and grabbed Hunt on the upper arm and took him around the side of the truck.

"Now look here —" he started with his finger raised in Hunt's face.

Hunt swatted it away and said, "No. *You* look here. Get these prisoners out now. Let's do the deal. We're ready to go and I am not waiting anymore. You can explain to the President why seventeen prisoners died of thirst and heat stroke waiting on a runway. And why he is without his prize asset."

The Brigadier stopped cold. He stared at Hunt for a moment and then turned away and barked at his soldiers to get the prisoners down. The mercenaries climbed down gingerly. They were thin and dirty. A few smiled at him through their thick beards and matted hair and lined up shoulder to shoulder next to the truck.

Hunt nodded to Digger. VD walked Sir William out into the sunlight. The Director of Intelligence closed his eyes and shaded them with his arm. He got a nudge in the back and walked down the stairs. VD stopped him at the base. He had a pistol sticking Sir William subtly in the ribs.

"How are we going to do this, Brigadier?" Hunt asked.

"You will release your prisoner and then I will release mine," he said and smiled broadly for the camera.

"No way," Hunt said, and the Brigadier's smile vanished. "We'll load sixteen of the prisoners. On the final one, we will each let our man go. You drive away. And then the deal will be complete."

The Brigadier thought for a moment. He looked very aware of the film crew. He nodded. His shoulders drooped. Hunt didn't miss a beat. He immediately started coaxing them down and guided the captured mercenaries up to the stairs. He helped one or two as they struggled to walk, their feet swollen and bruised from the beatings. Digger encouraged them on the way up, "Come on lads, in you come. Hot tea and biscuits waiting for you. In you come ..."

Hunt recognised a few of the lads as they passed him, a few nodded quietly and tipped imaginary hats and said, "Boss." When the second to last man went into the aircraft there was an air of stillness, of quiet. This was the moment of truth.

Each man outside the aircraft stood and looked at one another. Flies buzzed in the hot sun and a soldier swatted one away from his face. VD jabbed Sir William in the back and he took an involuntary step forward. Sir William tried to resist and the Brigadier waved at his soldiers to grab him. As they moved toward him, Hunt went and grabbed the last mercenary prisoner.

"Major Saint-John Price, retired," he said in shock, as Hunt pulled him to the aircraft.

"Nice to meet you," Hunt said as he pushed him up the stairs. Hunt turned back, the camera being following Sir William into the front seat of the Jeep. The Brigadier gave a lazy salute and smiled. Hunt nodded, and then said, "Come on VD let's get out of here."

VD hurried up the stairs and into the plane. Hunt followed him.

"Wait until they have gone, don't lower your weapon until they have," Hunt said to Digger, and he replied, "Aye-aye."

Hunt looked at the sorry state of humanity aboard the private jet. They were sprawled out, not enough seats for everyone. They sat in the aisle and two to a chair. They looked relieved and happy. Digger pulled up the stairs, "They're leaving," he said.

"Get us out of here, captain," Hunt shouted to the pilot. He heard the engines whine and the captain came over the speaker. Hunt sat in the jump seat like an air hostess and put his head back as the plane taxied down the runway and out of Africa.

CHAPTER THIRTY-EIGHT

OXFORDSHIRE, UNITED KINGDOM

It was night when they landed at RAF Brize Norton. They were greeted by flashing blue lights on top of black transporters. Customs Agents and Military Police surrounded the aircraft. Hunt looked out the window at the blue lights flashing through the rain. Ambulances waited behind the police.

Digger dropped the stairs and put his hands up.

"Put your hands up, drop your weapons, come out with your hands up!"

"Christ! Make up your minds, do you want me to put my hands up or drop my weapons?" Digger looked back at Hunt and winked.

"See you on the other side, Boss," he said and stepped down.

Hunt shook VD's hand.

"See you soon brother," he said.

"Please, no, no more for me," VD said and grinned.

"I'll make sure they get you a private cell," Hunt tapped VD on the arm.

Hunt was arrested, hooded and taken to an interrogation cell. No one spoke to him. He was left alone with his thoughts for a few hours, until finally he called out, "Come on Gerry, I know you are behind that glass looking at me. Don't you think I have stewed enough? I need to go and have a hot shower. It has been a hell of a few weeks ..."

Hunt sat quietly for another five minutes. Then there was a jingle of keys and the door to the interrogation room opened. Soames was standing in the doorway. The two men looked at one another for a few moments. Soames stepped in. He gestured to the guard to remove Hunt's handcuffs. Soames shook his head at Hunt while he rubbed his wrists, and then closed the door behind the guard.

"My God," Soames said. "What the hell have you done!"

Hunt was quiet. He felt tired. He needed Soames to think it through, and come to terms with where they were.

"I completed the mission, Gerry."

"Bloody hell! And then some! What am I supposed to do with you?"

"Go on, just tell me what *they* are going to do to me? Tried under the Official Secrets Act? Hanged from a yardarm until dead ...?"

Soames guffawed.

"No, I don't think so," he said and perched on the edge of the interview table. "They want to keep this quiet. It is a public relations nightmare. They are going to spin it so that it looks like Sir William gave himself up willingly in exchange for the prisoners. He will be a hero and the British establishment will put their full diplomatic weight behind a resolution to have him pardoned, freed, and then watch him sail off into the sunset."

"Minus a few toenails, no doubt," Hunt said, and almost smiled.

"You've either created, or saved, the agency from a severe embarrassment," Soames said, "And we don't know which, yet."

"In the meantime ...?"

"In the meantime, I have been asked to head up The Clubhouse ..."

Soames grinned his Churchillian-bulldog grin and jutted his jaw forward. Hunt saw the twinkle in his eye.

"Congrats, old man. Couldn't have happened to a nicer guy."

This time Hunt smiled.

"Oh, bugger off!" Soames said.

They laughed.

"This isn't going to be without consequences," Soames said. He was serious again. "You'd better lay low. I don't know if we will be able to keep you on the books or not."

"I never wanted to be on the books, Gerry. You know that. I only did this —"

"You did this because this is exactly what you were born to do. You did this because you think you need to find your-self, or about yourself, out there," he waved his arm and gestured to the outside world, "But, what you are too damn thick to realise, is that all you need to know about, and all you need to care about, is what is already in here."

Soames punched Hunt gently in the chest.

"Just, not in *here*, unfortunately," Soames said and tapped himself on the head. "You're as thick as they come."

"Pretty though ..."

"Bah!"

They were quiet, contemplative.

"Listen," Soames said, "This won't be the last of this. They will make a song and dance, but the reality is, they got caught with their hands in the cookie jar. You are going to take some heat. Just take it on the chin. You might be suspended. Extended holiday ... You can go and look for that thing you've been searching for?"

Hunt shrugged. He couldn't think about it right then.

"Maddy safe?"

"She is," Soames said. "So are the rest of the expedition. And Lord Langdon. Terrible stuff they went through, but as I understand it from the debriefs they have someone to thank for pulling them out of the muck."

Hunt glared at Soames.

"I know, I know. You're thinking we shouldn't have put them in the muck in the first place. But, you know .... The greater good and all that."

"You have a mole in The Clubhouse, Gerry. You need to flush them out."

"We're dealing with it."

There was a knock at the door and Soames half-turned.

"Right," he said, "I'd better leave them to it. Whatever they say, you did a hell of a job. Proper stuff, Hunt. Come and see me when they let you go and we can talk about your holiday plans ..."

They shook hands and Soames patted Hunt on the shoulder. Hunt watched as Soames left the room, and a group of UK Customs Agents in blue knitted tops and holding clipboards waited to enter. They had stern looks on their faces and nodded to Soames as he walked past. What did they think they could do to him after all of this?

Hunt started to laugh. The Customs men looked confused.

"Get in here boys, I'll tell you all about it ..."

GET EXCLUSIVE STIRLING HUNT NEWS

Would you like to stay in touch about my writing and receive free and exclusive updates?

Sign up to my Readers' Club now, and I will send you a **complimentary copy** of the Stirling Hunt novella **Dangerous Cargo**. Based on a true story.

Just tell me where to send it at:
www.stewartclydeauthor.com

Thanks for reading!

A REVIEW REQUEST

Thank you for sharing this adventure with me.

Many people are involved in publishing a book, but none are as important as you. If you enjoyed any of my novels, and have five minutes, could I ask you to please write a short review?

Your opinion matters to me, and reviews are extremely important to authors, because they help fellow readers find and share books they love! And they keep me writing ...

If you have five minutes, please press the link, or button below to leave a review: www.amazon.com

Thank you.

Stewart Clyde

ABOUT THE AUTHOR

Stewart Clyde is a former British Army Officer and current Amazon Charts bestselling author. He has a degree in Politics & International Relations. After graduation, he moved from South Africa to London and joined the army. He's lived in eight countries, including the United States, Germany, Thailand and Scotland, and travelled to over forty. After almost a decade in the Armed Forces, he resigned his commission to write. He likes adventures, and riding motorcycles through the wine routes of the Iberian Peninsula and the Western Cape. What he enjoys most is hearing from readers, please get in touch by visiting his website, or on social media.

For more please visit:
www.stewartclydeauthor.com

Join the Stewart Clyde Author Page
on your favourite social media

Printed in Great Britain
by Amazon

22697399R00145